F-Fr   FRASER, ANTHEA
1977   Breath of
c.1   brimstone.

6.95

3/77

Breath of Brimstone

ANTHEA FRASER

Breath of Brimstone

DODD, MEAD & COMPANY
NEW YORK

1 2 3 4 5 6 7 8 9 10

Library of Congress Cataloging in Publication Data

Fraser, Anthea.
  Breath of brimstone.

  I. Title.
PZ4.F8413Br3 [PR6056.R286] 823'.9'14   76–54325
ISBN 0–396–07405–7

Breath of Brimstone

CHAPTER 1

ON the day it all began, Celia woke with a heavy but indefinable sense of foreboding. Even the early morning sunshine pouring through the window held a hint of menace, as though implying that before darkness fell that night events would have been put in train which would totally destroy the pleasant tenor of her life. She shivered involuntarily and closed her eyes, trying to hold the approaching day at bay, but already Tom was beginning to stir beside her.

"What time is it?"

"I don't think it's seven yet."

"Hadn't you better check? I've this meeting at nine."

Reluctantly, since there was no help for it, she opened her eyes and reached for the clock. "Just after six."

"Good lord, the middle of the night!" He turned on his side and humped the sheet over his shoulder.

"Tom—" She was wide awake now.

"Um?"

"There isn't anything—unpleasant scheduled for today, is there?"

"There's the preterm staff meeting. That could be unpleasant enough, in all conscience."

"No, seriously. I can't get it out of my mind that some—"

"Look, love, do we have to hold a conversation at this ungodly hour? Go back to sleep, there's a good girl." And, untroubled by her presentiment, he slept.

But for Celia sleep was now beyond recall. It was the last week of the long summer holidays. Tom and the children returned to school next week and soon after that, with the departure of the last of the visitors, Rychester would thankfully revert to its civilized, out-of-season self. At last she would be able to go shopping without having to fight her way through hordes of dawdling holiday-makers, to walk when she felt like it along a pleasantly deserted promenade with the spray in her face and the wind in her hair and only the wheeling gulls for company. Far from being threatening, the days ahead were surely to be welcomed. But once again something cold and unknown reached out for her, negating her self-assurances.

"Tom," she began urgently, but his heavy breathing was her only answer. Silently she slipped out of bed and made her way to the bathroom. From the girls' room came the muted tones of a disc-jockey, followed by the subdued blare of the latest pop record. Kate had been forbidden to turn on her radio before seven in case she disturbed Lucy, but any attempt to remonstrate with her now would simply create more disturbance.

Celia leant over the bath and turned both taps on full, previewing the day with forced calm. Tom would be out till mid-afternoon. Kate had tennis coaching this morning and was invited out to tea this afternoon. Lucy no doubt had arranged to play with Julie as usual. The unaccustomed peace would give her a chance to bottle some fruit and make the tomato chutney she'd been meaning to do for weeks. A pleasant, useful day lay ahead. It was ridiculous to imagine otherwise.

2

By eight-fifteen the smell of frying bacon had tempted the children downstairs in their dressing-gowns and Tom was on his second cup of coffee, hidden behind the *Telegraph*.

"Still no definite date for the election. I can't imagine why they need to be so all-fired secretive about it. Perhaps they're afraid the entire population will flee if given too much warning—and who could blame us?"

"Pass Lucy the marmalade, dear," Celia said mechanically, seeing her younger daughter begin to reach forward to the imminent danger of the coffee pot. Tom folded the paper and glanced at his watch.

"Have you many new staff this term?" she asked idly.

"Not enough, as usual. Sue Carlton's baby's due at the beginning of November, but she's nobly promised to stay on a little longer to give us more chance of finding a replacement. If we can't, heaven help the poor kids doing O-level music. I've been lying awake for months worrying about it but I can't see what more I can do. God, I'd sell my soul for a really first-class music teacher!"

The sun slid behind a cloud and subconsciously they all registered its withdrawal. The little girls pulled their gowns more closely about them and Celia took a drink of hot coffee.

"I was hoping Lucy could start piano lessons this term," she remarked after a moment.

"Not a chance, as things are. Well, I suppose I'd better go." He bent to kiss the top of her head. "Have a good day. With luck I should be back about four." The door closed behind him.

"Go and change into your tennis things, Kate, or you won't be ready when Jenny calls. And do try not to lose any more balls."

"Today's a funny sort of colour," Lucy remarked, staring out of the window with her eyes screwed up, "all kind of hot

3

and exciting, with yellow and red stripes running into each other."

Celia looked across at her reflectively. Lucy had a positive obsession with colour. Not only did she insist that each day of the week and each month of the year had a distinctive colour of its own, but she was uncannily adept at gauging the moods of the family by means of what she called their "coloured lights." On the whole they played along with her, apart from the occasional superior scoffing from Kate. "I suppose it's the bright sunshine," she offered now.

Lucy shook her head. "No, it's nothing to do with the weather. I've never seen a day like this before. The colours are all—all jigging up and down."

"She means vibrating," said Kate loftily over her shoulder as she left the room.

"Well, vibrating or jigging or whatever they're doing, will you please go and get dressed. Is Julie calling for you?"

"Yes, she said after breakfast."

"Then hurry, it's after breakfast now."

"Not after Julie's breakfast. She doesn't get up early in the holidays."

"Don't pick at your finger, dear, you'll only make it sore. Off you go then and let me clear the table."

She wouldn't admit to herself that Lucy's unorthodox description of the day in any way tallied with her own. And yet—"I've never seen a day like this," she'd said. Suppose after all it *was* different, something out of the ordinary? Celia gave herself a little shake. It was as ludicrous to concede that Lucy really saw abstract colours as it was to give credence to her own nebulous apprehensions. Pushing it all to the back of her mind, she loaded the dishwasher and began to sort out the tomatoes.

*   *   *

4

"Hello? Anyone home?"

Celia pushed the hair back from her face and turned from the bubbling pans. "In the kitchen, Angie."

Her sister appeared in the doorway. "Goodness, you do look industrious! And what a heavenly smell!"

"It's bringing in all the wasps," Celia said ruefully. "Like some coffee? I'll be glad of an excuse to stop for a while."

"Lovely. It's certainly very peaceful. Where are the children?"

"Lucy's playing with Julie and Kate's at the Tennis Club."

"Lucky you. I left Eva and our two mooching round the house in their pyjamas. Thank goodness Ruth at least will be back at school next week."

"But you'll have Martin under your feet for another month or so yet."

Her sister's mouth tightened. "As a matter of fact, we look like having him indefinitely."

Celia turned, kettle in hand. "What do you mean?"

Angie flicked viciously at the wheel of her lighter. "We've just had the father and mother of a row. He calmly informed us over breakfast that he doesn't intend to take up his scholarship to Oxford."

"*What?*"

"I know. It's quite incredible." Angie drew quickly on her cigarette. "I've never seen Michael so angry. And of course the more furious he got, the more stubborn it made Martin, until I could cheerfully have knocked their heads together."

"But I don't understand. You mean he's not going to university at all?"

"That's what he tells us. He's —what's the accepted phrase?—'dropped out.' "

"But he's never even been 'in,' " Celia returned with a touch of grim humour. She poured coffee into the two cups.

5

"Really, though, I just can't believe it. He's had his heart set on it for so long."

"I know. I'm just about frantic. After all these years of congratulating ourselves on having bright offspring, suddenly, wham! Ruth flounders hopelessly with her O's and now this."

"And what *does* Martin intend to do?"

"As little as possible, from what I can gather. He may drift over to France, he says, and work his way around. Don't ask me how. It wouldn't be quite so bad if he'd simply changed his mind and had something else definitely lined up but he's so maddeningly vague and noncommittal."

"And all this came as a complete surprise?"

"Entirely. Oh, he's been a bit morose lately. He makes a point of never answering the first time you call him, things like that. And all he wants to do is lounge about the house all day playing records and hobnobbing with Eva." She looked across the table. "Which really brings me to the main reason for my visit."

"Oh?"

"Celia, with all this going on, Eva really is the last straw!"

"Eva is? But I thought—"

"You thought she would settle down marvellously, that she's so sweet and helpful and more or less inconspicuous anyway. Yes, so did I. Until she came."

"And what went wrong?"

Angie gave a harsh laugh that was more like a sob. "After what I've been telling you, you ask me that?"

"But you can hardly blame Eva for—"

"I'm not so sure. There's nothing I can put a finger on, of course, but then there wouldn't be, would there? Not with sweet, butter-wouldn't-melt Eva!"

The vindictiveness in her sister's voice astonished Celia.

6

"For heaven's sake, Angie, whatever has she done?"

"Well, for one thing I don't like her and Martin being thrown together so much. I suppose I should have foreseen something like this happening, but like a fool I didn't. Damn it all, the girl is my sister. Stepsister, anyway."

"You don't think she's a good influence on him?"

"I'm damn sure she isn't. They're always together these days. Once when I went into the sitting-room unexpectedly they were huddled together on the sofa. Martin went scarlet and sprang to his feet. Heaven knows what she'd been up to."

Celia said drily, "Martin's nearly nineteen, Angie. Almost a year older than Eva, in fact."

"But she's his *aunt!* It—it isn't decent!"

"In point of fact she's not a blood relation at all."

"Then I suppose I brought it on myself by having her, but what else could I do? Anyway, I've now got to the stage when I don't like leaving them alone in the house. I only came out now because Ruth's at home too."

"Obviously you can't go on like that," Celia said a little uncomfortably.

"Obviously. And as if that's not enough, I shouldn't be surprised if she were behind this sudden decision to opt out of Oxford."

"But why on earth?"

"I don't *know,* dammit. Perhaps she just wants him hanging around waiting on her." Angie inhaled deeply, swallowing the smoke. "As you know, Ruth has never liked her. It's largely resentment, I imagine, being made to feel left out when the other two are together. And although it's probably entirely without foundation, she quite openly blames Eva for her O-level results. Says Eva made a point of needling her every morning before the exams, so that she left the house fuming and couldn't concentrate on the papers. I must admit

7

I never noticed anything, but then, as I said, you don't, with Eva. All you see are the results of her—machinations."

"You seriously think she set out to make Ruth fail her exams and turn Martin away from Oxford?"

"Celia, I don't know *what* to think. All I do know is that until she came last year we were a happy, united family with no hangups. And since then, things have begun to go wrong —countless little things, that have culminated in these two big failures."

Celia stirred her coffee thoughtfully and the warm, spice-filled kitchen was quiet except for the ticking clock and the soft plopping from the pans. Her mind went back across the years to the dark-eyed two-year-old who had joined their family along with Father's second wife, beautiful Hungarian Irenka. Alan and Angie were both already married and living in Rychester and when, three years later, Celia married Tom, a boyhood friend of her brother, Alan had written to tell them of a vacancy for a master at the local school. So they too moved down to the south coast, three hundred miles from the family home, and since their father appeared completely wrapped up in his new wife and stepdaughter, visits between them became less and less frequent. None of them had really known the adolescent Eva, although after Irenka's death four years ago, she and their father had been down to stay with them all more often than previously. Then, last year, Father himself died, leaving a request that his family look after Eva. As the elder daughter and with a girl of her own only two years younger, Angie had automatically complied. This was Celia's first intimation that the arrangement had not been an unmitigated success.

Angie stirred and leant forward to stub out her cigarette. "I suppose you've gathered what I'm trying to say."

"You want us to have her here?"

"Could you possibly give it a try? It would at least give us a breathing space to get our two sorted out a bit. And if she does get you down, then of course we'll take her back. I feel awful asking, especially when you already have old Mrs. Bannerman on your hands."

"Oh, she's no trouble. She makes a great thing of being independent. Everything is arranged over the phone"—she nodded toward the intercom on the kitchen wall—"just as if she lived at the other end of town. She wouldn't dream of popping in unannounced. The only set time we have for seeing her is Sunday lunch. Sometimes I feel a bit guilty that we don't see more of her, but it was she who insisted that the flat should be completely self-contained, even to the outside staircase to her own front door. It terrifies me to think of her negotiating it, particularly in the winter when it's all icy, but she's a spry old thing and she goes up it like a two-year-old." She hesitated. "I'd like to help about Eva, Angie, but of course I can't say anything definite until I've spoken to Tom." She smiled fleetingly. "I don't suppose you even considered asking Alan and Melanie?"

Angie gave a snort of laughter. "Too right I didn't. Melanie would have developed one of her famous migraines at the very idea, though heaven knows you'd think she'd be glad of the company, with Alan out till all hours and Robert away at medical school." She hesitated. "If Tom agrees, we'll have to be tactful about it all. I don't want to hurt the girl's feelings, but I really do have to put my own two first. No doubt it'll occasion another blazing row with Martin, in any event. Well, I must go. I've still all the shopping to do. Give me a ring later when you've talked it over and let me know what Tom thinks."

As it happened, when he returned that afternoon Tom was too full of his own news to give Celia a chance to mention hers. He came bursting into the house, caught her round the waist and spun her into a crazy little dance.

"Guess what, my love! Our prayers have been answered! The most fantastic chap turned up today, completely out of the blue, and said he'd heard we were looking for a music master! He has a list of qualifications as long as your arm and can start straight away at the beginning of term. Can you beat that? So young Lucy can have her lessons after all, though they'll probably have to be fitted in after school—he has a pretty full timetable. Lord, the relief! I can hardly believe it!"

Before he had finished telling her all about the staff meeting Lucy came home and the question of Eva had to be shelved until the children were in bed. In the meantime Celia had been trying to think of the best way to broach the subject. She wanted to help her sister, who was obviously overwrought, but she also felt a sneaking sympathy for Eva. Angie, kind-hearted though she basically was, could be difficult at times, particularly where her children were concerned. Tom always maintained he would pity their eventual marriage partners, since Angie was sure to change overnight into the archetypical mother-in-law. And thirdly, Celia still remembered with warm nostalgia the doe-eyed child that Eva had once been.

Accordingly, when the door closed behind Kate *en route* for bed, she said at once, "Angie was here this morning. They've a problem on their hands with Martin: he's apparently refusing to go to Oxford after all."

"Martin is?" Tom looked at her in amazement.

"And Angie feels that Eva may be partly to blame."

He laughed shortly. "Isn't that carrying it a bit too far? I mean, I quite appreciate that Angie's loth to admit it could possibly be Martin's fault, but dragging Eva in! Heavens, the child hardly ever opens her mouth! What possible bearing could she have on anything?"

"Apparently they've been spending a lot of time together and Angie doesn't think it's a good thing."

"You want to know my opinion?" He poured himself another drink. "I think Angie, and Michael too, to some extent, have pushed those kids from the word go. They always had to be that much better than everyone else and quite suddenly they've both dug their heels in. It's a natural enough reaction. Ruth flunked her O's and Martin decided he's not after all cut out to be Archbishop of Canterbury or whatever it was his mother had mapped out for him."

Celia smiled. "You could be right, but the point is this. She wants to know if we'll take Eva, for a while at least."

"So she can blight our children's lives too? How kind!"

"You've just scotched that theory. And actually she's always been very good with Lucy, you've said so yourself."

"How do you feel about it, then? It would fall mainly on your shoulders."

"I wouldn't mind giving it a try. I thought the world of her when she was little; she was such a quaint, old-fashioned little thing. And she starts teacher training college next month, so she'd be out all day like the rest of you."

"Personally I can't say I'm overfond of the girl myself. She always has the effect of making me uncomfortable somehow, as though all the time she's apologizing for being there and hoping she's not disturbing anyone. It gets you down after a while."

"I think it's just that she's so painfully shy. After all, she doesn't really know any of us all that well. Most girls her age and in her circumstances would have opted for digs or a bed-sitter or something. I think it's rather pathetic, really, that she clings to the family because that was what Father wanted. I'd like to try to bring her out of her shell a bit."

"Okay, it's up to you. But she comes on the strict understanding that if it doesn't work out or you change your mind, we return her to Angie. After all, if her dark suspicions do have any foundation, it would hardly benefit my career for my own daughters to fail their O-levels!"

Celia laughed. "Thanks. I'll phone and tell her in the morning. I don't know that Eva's removal will make any difference to Martin's plans but at least it'll give Angie a break. Now that's settled I'll go and see to the dinner."

"Oh, by the way," Tom called after her, "I've invited this new chap for Sunday lunch. You don't mind, do you?"

She halted abruptly, her brain whirling with panic excuses even as she tried helplessly to analyze her strong but inexplicable antipathy to the suggestion.

"It seemed the only decent thing to do," Tom went on. "After all, he doesn't know anyone round here yet. Incidentally, he was very interested to hear that you'd studied music yourself." And, at her continuing silence, he added with a touch of impatience, "All right?"

"Your mother might not be too pleased," she said at last with an effort. "You know she regards family lunch on Sunday as her special prerogative."

"She won't mind for once."

It seemed pointless to argue any further. In any case, the invitation had already been extended. Uneasily she went through to the kitchen to prepare the meal.

It was not until she switched off the bedside light that Celia again remembered the curious sense of approaching trouble with which she had awakened that morning. With a pleasant sense of danger averted, she told herself that of course it had all been nonsense. It had been a perfectly normal day and nothing very terrible had happened after all.

12

She was drifting off to sleep when another thought occurred to her.

"Tom, are you awake?"

"Um? What is it?"

"You didn't tell me his name."

"Whose name?"

"The music master's, who's coming to lunch on Sunday."

"Oh, rather an unusual name, really. Lucas Todd."

"Lucas Todd," she repeated sleepily, and as the name dropped into her mind, total blackness overcame it and she slept.

CHAPTER 2

CELIA phoned Angie the next morning to arrange for Eva to move in with them on Saturday. "And why don't you all come for lunch on Sunday?" she added on the spur of the moment. "It may help to dispel any idea that you're washing your hands of her. Tom has invited a new member of staff as well, so we'll be quite a party. I'll ask Alan and Melanie too."

Only later, as she bustled about the house preparing Eva's room and sorting out the children's school uniforms, did it strike her that her gathering of the family about her had been an instinctive act of self-preservation, presenting a united front to the intruder. She promptly discounted the idea, together with the aversion she had felt when Tom first mentioned the man's coming. Her foreboding on Wednesday had proved completely unfounded. So, no doubt, would this one.

Michael duly delivered Eva and her luggage during the course of Saturday morning and Celia hurried out to welcome them, the sight of Eva's small, rather forlorn figure underlining Tom's ridicule of the suspicions Angie had levelled against her.

"Eva darling, how lovely to see you! We're so looking forward to having you with us!" The girl submitted silently to her embrace, eyes downcast and a slight smile on her lips.

14

"Michael, if you could just put her cases in the hall, Tom will take them up later." Her glance returned a shade doubtfully to Eva, who still had not spoken. She was standing with lowered eyes and hands demurely clasped in front of her for all the world like a Victorian governess. It struck Celia for the first time that Eva never wore bright colours, seeming to prefer greys and browns which merged into the background. Nor did she bother with makeup, and the creamy pallor of her skin was dominated by her huge dark eyes and the thick, heavy fringe of black hair cut uncompromisingly straight across her forehead. She reminded Celia uncomfortably of a displaced mid-European refugee, which, in a manner of speaking, she was. Hard on the thought, Celia tucked her arm through Eva's and led her into the house. Lucy came flying down the length of the hall to greet them and for the first time the girl's face came alive as she bent to catch the excited child.

"Oh Eva, I'm *so* glad you're coming to live with us! Come up and see your bedroom! It's next door to me and Kate but it's up some little steps all by itself." She caught hold of Eva's hand and, with a half-laughing, half-apologetic glance over her shoulder, the girl allowed herself to be pulled up the stairs.

"You've time for a sherry, haven't you, Michael?"

"That would be very pleasant. Thanks." He followed her into the long drawing-room, warm now in the rays of the midday sun. "Actually, I must admit I'm in no hurry to go home. The atmosphere at the moment leaves a lot to be desired. No doubt Angie told you Martin's being extremely difficult? I'm not even sure whether he'll grace your table at lunch tomorrow. At the moment he's not speaking to any of us."

"Because of Eva leaving?"

15

"Partly, of course, but some hard things were said the other day when he dropped his bombshell. Mind you, he's been getting progressively more bloody-minded for months. I'm forced to admit he's hardly in the right frame of mind at the moment to read theology!"

"I was so sorry to hear about it all. It must be a terrible disappointment for you." She handed him the glass. "Here's to a happy solution to your problems!"

"Thanks, I'll drink to that. And to a peaceful rehabilitation for Eva, not to mention the rest of you."

"Do you really think she'd anything to do with all the trouble?"

"Search me. Martin's certainly enamoured of her at the moment, but from what we can see it's all on his side and she's given him no encouragement. In fact, it would be difficult to find a more passive character than young Eva. She speaks only when spoken to, and for the most part fades so completely into the background that I have to keep reminding myself that she's there. How does Tom feel about having her?"

"He more or less left it to me, though he did say she made him feel uncomfortable. He should be back any minute, if you'd like to wait."

"Actually I'd better not stay too long. It's hardly fair on Angie. She's taken all this pretty hard, as you may have gathered. In a way it does seem unfair, her kindness in taking Eva rebounding on her in this way."

"If Eva had anything to do with it," Celia put in quietly.

He gave a laugh. "Innocent until proved guilty. Quite right. As a solicitor I shouldn't need reminding of the maxim." He drained his glass. "Thanks for the liquid refreshment. What time do you want us tomorrow?"

Tomorrow! She moistened her lips, one finger rubbing

agitatedly against the hard little lump of skin on her index finger. "About twelve, I should think."

"And you'll understand if there are only three of us?"

"Of course, but I hope Martin does decide to come."

They moved into the hall and Celia called, "Michael's just going, Eva." She and Lucy appeared at the top of the stairs.

"Goodbye, Michael, and thank you."

"Bye, Eva, I hope you settle down all right. I'm sure you will," he added with a forced heartiness which cast doubt rather than otherwise on the sentiment.

"Bring Eva down now, Lucy," Celia instructed. "She can't unpack till Daddy takes her cases upstairs and she may like a sherry before lunch." She waved Michael goodbye, closed the front door and turned to the two girls coming down the stairs, Lucy still chatting animatedly.

"And tomorrow," she was saying, "instead of just Grandma coming for dinner we're having a party. Auntie Angie and Uncle Michael, and Martin and Ruth, and Uncle Alan and Auntie Melanie, and a man who's going to give me piano lessons."

Fleetingly an expression of such intensity crossed Eva's face that Celia caught her breath, but it was gone in the same instant, leaving her wondering if she had imagined it. It was in any case indescribable, a split-second revelation of a depth of emotion beyond her own comprehension. But all the girl said, quietly, was, "That should be fun."

Slowly Celia followed them into the drawing-room, her mind shifting with unwelcome conjectures. It was with a sense of thankfulness that she heard the front door open again and Tom's voice in the hall.

The next morning she awoke to the sound of church bells and in her sleep-drugged brain their carillon sounded an

17

urgent alarm. She thought confusedly: if only no one was coming to lunch we could all go to church this morning. It seemed a long time since she and Tom had been. For a moment the desire to go was overwhelming, but of course as it happened a lot of people were coming to lunch. In fact— she did a rapid calculation—they would be thirteen at the table. At once her body jerked like an exposed nerve. Thirteen! If only she had checked the numbers before inviting Alan and Melanie! But as the ancient superstition hung heavily over her she thankfully remembered a possible reprieve. Michael had said that Martin might not come. Oh, please don't let him come! If he doesn't, everything might be all right after all.

Abruptly Celia opened her eyes and lay gazing at the ceiling. Whatever was the matter with her? All that gibberish about the bells and the number at table: She had never been superstitious before, yet this week even the most ordinary things had seemed pregnant with hidden meanings. It was probably just that she was tired at the end of the long school holidays. She resolved to try to rest a little next week, perhaps even to buy a tonic from the chemist.

However, her resting could not start today. A turkey had seemed the easiest way to feed such a multitude—not, she thought with a touch of self-mockery, being much of a hand with loaves and fishes—and by now the autotimer should already have switched on the oven. But there was still the melon to prepare for the first course and the last touches to be put to the giant trifle. She must remind Tom to carry the kitchen table through straight after breakfast to put end to end with the dining-room one. Before she could stop herself she wondered whether, if she left a slight gap between the tables, it would somehow cancel out the implication of their total number.

18

In exasperation she swung out of bed, determined to put an end to such nonsense, but nevertheless she closed the windows against the persistent chiming of the bells. "Tom, there's a lot to do this morning. Go down like a love and put the kettle on while I have a quick bath." Leaving him grumbling she hurried out of the room and away from her childish fancies.

The moment Eva appeared at the breakfast table, Celia was painfully aware of the extreme tension in her. "What fun" she had said, when told by Lucy of the luncheon party. But would it in fact be fun for such a pathologically shy girl to be exposed to a crowd of people, even if it was largely composed of members of her adopted family? Celia began to regret her own selfishness in subjecting the girl to an avoidable ordeal so soon after the disruption of her life at Angie's.

"You'll know everyone, of course, except Mr. Todd," she told her rallyingly, pitying the quiver which crossed the pale face before, obediently, Eva managed a brief smile. "And if you want to escape to your room after the meal no one will mind. Not that I want you to," she added hastily, detecting a possible misunderstanding, and again her only reward was that tight, fleeting smile, more a contortion of the facial muscles than a sign of pleasure.

By twelve o'clock Celia's nerves were as tightly strung as Eva's. She stood in the center of the kitchen with icy hands clasped together, furiously asking herself what it was that she feared. In the oven the turkey, brown and crisp and surrounded by pink tongues of bacon, was cooked to perfection. The first of the season's sprouts, firm and tightly curled, were ready for the pan. Stuffing, bread sauce, potatoes. Mentally she checked the list. On the elongated dining table, its join covered by overlapping cloths, the slices of melon lay waiting, artistically if somewhat liberally decorated with cherries by an enthusiastic Kate. And on the sideboard reposed the bowl of trifle, redolent of sherry beneath its coverlet of cream. Please let everything be all right! she thought in agitation. And then, despicably, and please don't let Martin come!

But the first ring at the doorbell dashed her tentative hopes. Angie and Michael stood on the step with both children beside them. At least, Celia told herself, leading them to the drawing-room where her own family awaited their guests, Martin's presence might help to relax Eva. He was a good-looking boy, tall and fair, and he went straight to join her, his six feet towering protectively over her diminutive figure. Before she had a chance to gauge Eva's own reaction, the bell sounded again and this time it was Mrs. Bannerman who waited outside.

"Really, Mother"—Celia kissed her perfumed cheek with an equal mixture of affection and exasperation—"how many times do we have to tell you there's no need for you to ring?"

The older woman smiled serenely. "I hear we are a rather extended number today?"

"Hello, Grandma." Kate stood on tiptoe for her kiss and behind them the front door opened without ceremony to reveal Alan's cheerful face.

"Greetings, gentlefolk! What a scrumptious smell!"

"Oh Kate," Celia said despairingly, "I did tell you to keep the kitchen door closed. Hello, Melanie, how are you?" She smiled dutifully at her sister-in-law, wondering as she did so whether life could really be such a burden as Melanie always made out. They moved past her in a body into the drawing-room, greeting the others already there. Only one more guest still to come. A fit of trembling took hold of her—or perhaps it was shivering, for she was suddenly very cold. Weakly she leant against the wall, fighting to compose herself, and in that moment the doorbell jangled down the length of the hall, its warning even more explicit than that of the church bells earlier. Through the glass of the front door she could see the blurred outline of their last guest, but she completely lacked the propulsion to force her way down the hall to admit him. In fact she even found herself pressing farther back against the wall, unreasoningly convinced that his gaze had somehow penetrated the frosted glass of the door and he was witnessing her craven discomfiture.

Behind her Tom's voice said, "Oh, there you are. Wasn't that the bell? Wake up, England!" He patted her reprovingly, strode to the front door and flung it open. With a supreme act of will, Celia pushed herself away from the protective wall and moved up the hall toward him.

"Todd, this is my wife, Celia. Mr. Todd, darling, the answer to our prayers!"

"How do you do?" His voice was low and musical. He held out his hand and with the resignation of despair she put her own into it. It would have been hard to say which was the colder.

For Celia, the next few minutes were a jumbled blur. Somehow they had rejoined the others in the drawing-room —she did wish Eva wouldn't gaze quite so intently at Mr. Todd—and there was a glass in her hand. She drank from it quickly, before her shaking hand could spill its contents. The drink steadied her a little and she braced herself to look across the room to where Lucas Todd stood smiling down at Mrs. Bannerman. Seeing him now clearly for the first time, she attempted to fathom what had so disturbed her. At first glance there did not seem to be anything out of the ordinary about him. He was conventionally good-looking, his dark hair shaped fashionably into sideburns, his olive skin smooth and with an almost polished appearance. He was of only medium height, slightly built and with narrow shoulders, and although his hands and feet were small, she saw that he had the long, tapering fingers of the true musician.

She had reached this point in her inventory when he turned his head and she received the full impact of his gaze. Immediately her heart set up a frenzied tattoo high in her chest and her face grew hot. There was a deeply compelling quality about those strange, heavy-lidded eyes which affected her profoundly and she was blazingly aware of an animal magnetism about him which repelled even as it strongly attracted her. For a second longer those hooded eyes held her captive as effortlessly as a snake hypnotizing a rabbit. Then, carelessly releasing her, he turned away, bending down to Lucy and saying pleasantly, "Well, young lady, I hear you want to learn to play the piano."

Celia made her escape to the kitchen, cold hands pressed against fiery cheeks. What appalling arrogance! she thought furiously. How dared he subject her to so humiliating a display of his power—power which, until it claimed her, she had not even suspected. Fortunately no one seemed to have noticed the unspoken exchange—no one, that is, except Eva. For Eva, Celia knew, had not been listening to Martin's quiet conversation. All her attention had been riveted on the newcomer, although he had not, to Celia's knowledge, glanced in her direction.

Mechanically she put a light under the sprouts and potatoes, began gently to reheat the bread sauce. But how dare he, she thought again, come to her home and carelessly force her to acknowledge, within minutes of their meeting, the strength of his will? As the seconds lengthened, a measure of calm returned. Briefly she considered hurrying to the dining-room and rearranging the place cards. Tom would expect her to seat Lucas Todd on her right. Would he question the omission if she were to change it? But that would mean altering the whole table, which had been difficult to arrange in the first place due to the usual preponderance of females. Even more important was the distinct possibility that one of the children would remark on the change, since they had hopped excitedly after her as she laid the cards in position. It seemed she had no choice but to go through the meal with Lucas Todd beside her. At least Alan was immediately on her left if she should need him.

In the event, she did not. When she steeled herself to look in Mr. Todd's direction as they all filed through for lunch, it was to be greeted with a calm, almost gentle smile. This power was apparently something he could switch on and off at will. Having put her to the test, he was content for the moment to leave it in abeyance. She could only be grateful.

On her left Alan was grumbling happily about the deficiencies of the National Health Service. "One of these days I'll throw it all in and emigrate to America." It was a time-honoured threat. None of them believed him and he did not expect them to. On Lucas Todd's right, Angie made polite, rather stilted conversation. With half an ear, Celia listened to it; they were at the moment discussing their favourite composers. Instantly aware of her caught interest, Todd turned back to Celia.

"I believe you studied music yourself, Mrs. Bannerman. What instrument did you play?"

"The violin. I had intended to make a career of it but—well, I met Tom again and allowed myself to be distracted!"

"Tom was an old friend of mine," Alan put in from across the table. "The last time he'd seen Celia she was just a schoolgirl with pigtails. I suppose that would be back in '56, before he went to Canada. He went out as a newly qualified teacher on some exchange scheme and became so enamoured of it that he stayed five years. He probably wouldn't have come back at all but for the fact that his father died. He'd no other family and felt he owed it to his mother to come home."

"So Mr. Bannerman's gain was the music world's loss!" Lucas Todd said with a smile. Celia gave a disparaging little shrug and a smile, glancing down the length of the table at Tom. He seemed a long way away, engaged in being heavily patient with the latest of Melanie's complaints. "But now that the children are older," Lucas Todd continued, "perhaps you might take it up again?"

"I'm afraid it's too late now."

"Do you play the violin, Todd?"

"After a fashion, yes, but the piano has always been my instrument."

"You two will have to give us a Victorian-style musical evening one of these days!"

"I should be delighted, if Mrs. Bannerman agrees." Again the quality of his voice struck her. He spoke rather slowly, with perfect enunciation and a deep, melodious resonance so that even his most casual conversation held the attention of his listeners—which, she realized now, did not only include herself and Alan. Farther down the table, as still as a small grey statue, Eva sat with her eyes fixed devouringly on Lucas Todd.

The meal ended at last. The remains of the trifle lay in creamy ruins and the cheese plates were pushed aside.

"If you rub your finger so hard you will make it sore," Lucas Todd said softly, breaking into Celia's turbulent thoughts. Startled, she glanced at him and, following his eyes, down to her hand resting on the table.

"I know, it's a silly habit. I'm always telling Lucy not to do it but I'm as bad as she is." Rather self-consciously, aware of his attention still on her hand, she moved it to fold her

24

napkin and rose to her feet. "Let's go through for coffee, everyone." For the space of a second, before he too stood, he looked up at her and the curious current blazed briefly between them. His eyes had curious gold flecks in them, like an animal's. She tore herself free of them and the moment passed.

When they reached the drawing-room it was to find that heavy clouds were massing at the back of the house and the wind had risen. Out in the garden the trees threshed their branches, and a few dislodged leaves were floating prematurely to the ground. Angie helped to pass round the coffee cups and, to the family's slightly embarrassed amusement, Lucy reappeared with her autograph book and marched straight over to offer it to the music master.

"I must read what other people have written first," he procrastinated.

"I'm afraid there's nothing very inspired in it," Tom commented. "It's all strictly of the 'By hook or by crook' variety."

Lucas Todd smiled. "What would you like me to write, Lucy?"

The child hesitated for a moment. "A message," she said at last. Out of the corner of her eye, Celia saw Eva's hand clench convulsively and was aware of a spurt of irritation. What was the matter with the girl now?

The pen scratched briefly over the paper and he handed the book back to Lucy, who painstakingly read what he had written. When she looked up, there was a new interest in her eyes. "Yes," she said, "it does, doesn't it?"

"May I see?" Celia leant forward. The child held the book out for her and she read in a beautiful copperplate the single line: "Wishing will make it so" and underneath his signature and the date.

25

"Lucas Todd," Lucy said slowly, tracing the letters with her finger. "It's a funny name, isn't it? What does it mean?"

"Lucy," Celia began reprovingly, but he gave a soft laugh.

"As a matter of fact, it means almost the same as your name. Lucy means 'shining' and Lucas means 'light.' Lucy and Lucas—shining light."

Lucy clapped her hands delightedly. "So we really have the same name, one a man's and one a lady's?"

"Indeed we have." He smiled at her.

"Lucy," the child repeated, as though hearing her own name for the first time. "Lucy and Lucifer."

There was a moment's total silence. Then Kate, blessedly unaware of her sister's faux pas, demanded eagerly, "Does Kate mean light too?"

"No," he answered quietly. "As far as I remember, Kate —or Katherine—means 'pure.' "

"Oh." Obviously the explanation was an anticlimax.

"It's funny," Lucy said suddenly, "your name meaning 'light,' because you haven't got one."

"Oh Lucy!" groaned Tom. "Not all that again, please!"

"But he hasn't, Daddy. Everyone else has—you and Mummy and—"She broke off. Lucas Todd was leaning forward very slightly, looking down at her as she knelt at his feet with the autograph book on her lap.

"And what?" Michael prompted smilingly.

Lucy frowned. "I don't know. I've forgotten what I was going to say."

"Is there any more coffee, Celia?" Alan came forward with his cup and saucer. She found that her breath was coming very rapidly and made an effort to regulate it.

"Yes, of course." Out of the corner of her eye she saw Lucas bend down, his hand closing over Lucy's.

"Please leave that poor little finger alone!" His own finger,

26

long, bony and smooth, rubbed gently over the sore place as if to make it better.

When that night, after tossing and turning for what seemed an age, Celia at last fell asleep, she had an extraordinarily vivid dream. It seemed that Lucas Todd was standing immediately in front of her, his eyes looking deep into hers, wordlessly promising her an abundance of wonderful things. Then, slowly, he reached for her hand and gently lifted it, rubbing his finger over hers as he had over Lucy's and, glancing down, she saw without surprise that the little knot of hard skin had become a swollen purplish lump. Of its own accord her other hand went up to his face, stroking the smoothness of his jaw, his rather aquiline nose and the thick hair above his ears. Smilingly he caught hold of her hand and held it tightly with the other between his own. "Wishing will make it so," he said.

CHAPTER 3

THE dream was still with Celia at breakfast, inexplicable but somehow threatening, and although the day she had dreaded was behind her, she had a vague suspicion that it had not passed off as harmlessly as she had hoped. For one thing, the uncomfortable memory of her violent reaction to Lucas Todd caused her considerable disquiet. He had not chosen to exercise his power after that first confrontation, but she had no doubt that the bond forged between them in that single, searing glance would be resurrected as and when he chose and despairingly she doubted her ability to withstand it.

There was also a persistent cameo in her mind of him and Lucy, immobile, held timelessly together, his hand over hers as she knelt looking up at him. And lastly she was far from happy about Eva's strange behaviour at the luncheon party. Glancing at her across the table now, she noted that the pale lips were slightly compressed and there were purple shadows round the huge, habitually downcast eyes. Could Eva possibly imagine that she had fallen in love with the man? Apart, presumably, from their initial introduction, which Celia herself had been too distressed to register, she was not aware of his having paid her the slightest attention.

Tom's voice broke in on her musings. "Well, girls, it's the

last day of the holidays. How are you going to spend it?"

Kate said complacently, "Jenny's mother is taking us to the pictures—it's *Robin Hood*—and I'm going back to tea afterwards."

"It's not fair," pouted Lucy, "you went out to tea last week, too."

"And you're playing with Julie, no doubt?"

Lucy nodded. "Sometimes," she remarked candidly, "I get a bit tired of playing with Julie."

Tom laughed. "Never mind, you'll have plenty of companions starting tomorrow."

Only half listening, Celia let her eyes rest on her daughters. There was a grave, old-world quality about Kate's appearance, with her serious velvet-brown eyes and the heavy plaits which she wore forewards over her shoulders. She was a neat child, calmly aware of her own potentiality and content to work to realize it. Lucy, on the other hand, was at six years old barely past babyhood, still round-cheeked and blandly convinced of her undisputed right to everything she wanted. Occasionally the tenacity with which she clung to this belief worried her mother. She was fairer than Kate, Celia's colouring rather than Tom's, and her soft hair was caught up into a high ponytail which left vulnerable the tender nape of her neck. Celia ached with the intensity of her love for them and tried to rid her mind of the idea that some vague threat hung over them.

They were asking permission to leave the table and she nodded assent, including Eva in the release. "More coffee?" she asked Tom.

"Thanks, if it's still hot." He studied her face. "You all right, dear? You seem a bit subdued this morning."

"I had rather an unsettled night."

"Never mind, you'll be rid of us tomorrow and can take

things a bit more easily. When does Eva's term start?"

"I didn't think to ask. October, I imagine, like the universities."

"I don't suppose she'll be much trouble, especially as we have no teenaged sons mooning round the place! Incidentally, did you notice that she couldn't take her eyes off Todd yesterday? Young Martin had better look to his laurels!" He waited for her comment but she had none to offer and after a moment he added, "What did you think of him?"

She put her cup carefully down on its saucer. "Mr. Todd? He's rather a—strange man, isn't he?"

"Strange? I don't think so. Personally I found him charming, and I gathered that most of the female members of the family did too. I doubt if Eva was the only one smitten; he certainly had Lucy eating out of his hand!"

She moved abruptly. "Tom, I'm not so sure after all that it would be a good thing for him to give her piano lessons."

"You're not serious, surely? Good lord, if I could have chosen any tutor in the country for her I doubt if I'd have landed on a better one than Todd. And quite apart from that, there was an instant rapport between them."

She could hardly say that was what worried her. "Perhaps she's still a bit on the young side," she persisted desperately. "Let's leave it for a year and give her time to settle in more at school."

Tom laid down his cup, staring at her uncomprehendingly. "I can hardly believe my ears! You of all people talking of a child being *too young* to start music lessons! Look, if you think his qualifications are bogus or something, I can always arrange for you to hear him play. That will dispel any doubts you might have."

"I'm sure he's very good. It's just that she's so—" Vulnerable? Tom couldn't be expected to accept the applicability of the word.

"Of *course* she's young!" he broke in, thinking she had been about to repeat her first objection. "That's what's so wonderful about finding a man like this for her at the outset. It's the chance of a lifetime. It was your idea in the first place and having accepted it, I'm hanged if I'm going to back down now. What on earth would he think? Or Lucy herself, for that matter."

Celia was uneasily aware that it was something far more important than music lessons that she was fighting against with such undefined desperation, but she also realized that her fears were too vague to have any hope of convincing Tom.

He pushed his chair back. "I have to look in at the school for a while to make sure everything's ready for tomorrow. How about calling for me around twelve and we'll go out for lunch? We might even have a look at those curtains at Rawdons. I'm sure Eva wouldn't mind getting the kids their lunch. Kate will be out all afternoon anyway, and I imagine Lucy would relish being with Eva for a while. It will make a welcome change from the ever-present Julie!"

He bent to kiss her. "Okay? Cheer up, love, I don't like to see you so peaky. About twelve, then?"

She nodded. "All right, I'll be there."

"Shall I leave you the car?"

"No, you take it. I'll walk down through the park. The fresh air will do me good."

It was undeniably autumn. Although the sun, mellower than a month ago, was warm and strong, the night's heavy dew still lay on the grass, and twigs and branches were scattered untidily across the paths as evidence of the weekend's high winds. In the windows of the High Street, swim-suits and sunhats had given way to tweeds and the first of the autumn fashions. A few visitors still lingered in small groups, but with the approaching new term those with children had already returned home.

Celia crossed the broad road and turned into whimsically named Smugglers' Walk, which led down to Front Street. Today, however, she followed it only as far as Water Lane and Rychester High School. She hated the school buildings during the holidays, with their long echoing corridors and empty classrooms. It always made her think of Hamelin after the departure of the Pied Piper. She made her way quickly to Tom's study, tapped on the door, and had opened it before she realized he was not alone. Lucas Todd was leaning against the window frame, the sun behind him bestowing on him a dark, unholy halo. Immediately, her dream rushed to the front of her mind and she instinctively put both hands behind her back. From the amusement she detected in his eyes in that first quick glance, it almost seemed as though he had understood the gesture.

"Ah, there you are, dear." Tom rose unhurriedly to his feet. "We've just been going over Todd's timetable." His eyes held hers briefly, charging her not to repeat her objections. "It won't be possible to fit in Lucy's lessons during school hours, but he's quite amenable to giving them at home."

"But—we haven't a piano," she faltered stupidly.

"I have, Mrs. Bannerman." The amusement was still in his voice but at the same time it held an intimate caressing quality which raised the hairs on the back of her neck. "I understand from Mrs. Carlton," he was going on smoothly, "that it is the normal practice for pupils to attend lessons in the teacher's home after school or on Saturday mornings and I am quite prepared to continue this."

32

She moistened her lips. "You have found somewhere to live, then?"

"Yes, I have been fortunate enough to take over the lease of a handsome flat down on Front Street." He smiled. "I am full of admiration for the original town planners. They showed a most unusual imagination in building only on the inland side of the road. All those hotels and boarding houses can truthfully boast of 'sea views' even if we are too high up to have the benefit of the flower gardens down on the promenade."

"Yes, it's quite a drop from one level to the next," Tom agreed. "I've always maintained that it's the extreme steepness of our roads and the hilliness of the district generally that have spared us from becoming a kind of repository for the nation's senior citizens. In fact, unless you go right down to the end of Water Lane, which is a mile or more, the only way to reach the promenade is by way of the series of steep steps which lead down from Front Street."

"Yes, there is a flight almost opposite my flat. I have already made use of them."

"It must have been pretty wild down there during the weekend gales."

"I found it most exhilarating." He straightened. "But I am delaying your luncheon appointment."

"There's no hurry," Tom said quickly. "In fact, I wonder if I could ask you a favour? My wife is most anxious to hear you play, if you have a moment or two to spare."

"But of course." Lucas Todd's eyes moved slowly over her face, doubtless reading in it her repudiation of Tom's assertion. A smile touched his mouth. "I may say the desire is mutual." And as her eyes jerked to his face, he added, "However, I doubt if we have access to a violin."

She thought helplessly: he enjoys tying me in knots and

33

watching me flounder. I loathe, loathe, loathe him! But Tom's hand was lightly under her elbow and she went perforce with them down the long corridors to the music wing, cold now and damp-smelling after being closed up for two months.

"I don't guarantee the quality of the piano," Tom was saying apologetically. "As you can imagine, they all get hell beaten out of them. Let's try this one." He pushed open the solid, soundproofed door of one of the music cubicles. Dust lay thickly on the lid of the piano and a few dead wasps and flies littered the windowsill. "Obviously the cleaners haven't got this far yet."

"No matter." Lucas Todd moved lightly to the instrument, lifted the lid and trailed his long fingers lovingly over the keys. "What would you like to hear?"

"We'll leave the choice to you."

Tom motioned Celia to the only chair and she obediently sat down, resenting his insistence on hearing Lucas play. She didn't doubt he was good. He would excel at everything he undertook.

The music started, filling the small listening room. She recognized it in the opening bars—it was from Gounod's *Faust*—but his control of both music and instrument was something she had never experienced before. The sound seemed to reach out for her personally, to buffet and torment her beyond bearing. Suddenly her clothes prickled her skin, the wooden chair dug viciously into her back and she was aflame with feverish heat, itching all over in an agony of discomfort. As she twisted and turned on the hard seat vainly seeking a more comfortable position, the character of the music abruptly changed and began to flow over her like a vast soothing balm. It was as though it—or its player— was saying: If you fight me I can make you regret it.

34

If you succumb, there is nothing I will not do for you.

Blissfully at ease again she let herself relax and strange, exciting fancies began to pass through her mind. She saw herself, exquisitely gowned, seated on a concert platform before a wildly applauding crowd, an older, brilliantly gifted Lucy beside her; saw Tom, imposing and dignified in cap and gown, headmaster of a famous public school. Then it seemed that she was floating in warm tropical waters, gazing down at the sea-treasure of pebbles and strangely shaped shells scattered prodigally on the white sand of the ocean floor. There was a coral-ringed lagoon, a villa with shutters closed against the blazing noonday sun. In her confused state she accepted that all the most powerful desires she had known were being paraded before her for her recognition and acknowledgment. *They will be yours, if—*

She thought: How wonderful that Lucy will have the chance to learn music like this! She half turned to look up into Tom's face, but his eyes were glazed and staring. He seemed in a trance. What deep-hidden longings were being presented for his temptation? she wondered fleetingly. If only this glorious music need never end!

But end it did at last, and the sudden silence rushed in on their eardrums with the ferocity of an assault. She put a hand to her face and found it wet with tears. Tom moved at last, arching his stiff back. Lucas Todd had still not turned from the piano. What did one say? "That was very nice, thank you"? It would be an insult to offer any comment at all. Better by far to let their soul-shaken silence be his reward—and she knew he neither expected nor desired any other.

At last he turned and stood in one fluid movement, looking down consideringly at their white, dazed faces. "Perhaps you should go for lunch," he said gently. They nodded and, hand-in-hand like children, left the room with him still

35

standing by the piano which had so magnificently served him. Neither of them spoke until they were outside the school gates sitting in the car.

"Phew! I feel as though I'd been through a wringer!"

"It was—incredible," she said.

"I don't know about you but I need a drink. But badly."

There was another long silence between them which lasted until they were seated opposite each other in the dining-room of the Dragon Hotel.

"Wasn't that the most fantastic experience?" Tom exclaimed then. "I can't get over it! I presume that after that you haven't any more objections to Lucy starting with him?"

Vaguely she remembered during the music acquiescing joyously to the idea. But time was diluting the potency of the spell and she was in no doubt about its danger. "How do you think poor little Lucy would stand up to an onslaught like that?"

Tom smiled. "Oh, I don't imagine he'd subject the kids to that. At least, I hope not. That was his way of overcoming your resistance."

She stared at him sickly, amazed that he had recognized the ploy. "You were the one who offered to sell his soul for a music master. Perhaps *Faust* wasn't such a random choice."

He laughed. "Did I say that? Well, I admit I was desperate. Seriously, though, it was fabulous, wasn't it? I'd give my right arm to play like that!"

She said sharply, "Do stop making these extravagant claims, Tom. In any case, to be realistic about it, without your right arm you *couldn't* play like that."

He looked at her in surprise. "Don't be waspish, my love, it doesn't become you."

36

"Then can we change the subject? I've had as much as I can take of Lucas Todd for the moment."

"Very well, but you must allow me my moment of glory for having found him. Now, what shall we have to eat?"

The meal was enjoyable, the wine all it should be, but Celia had no appetite. Her traumatic experience had left her with a raging headache. She would have liked to go for a long, solitary walk along the promenade to restore her sanity, but Eva and Lucy awaited her at home and in any event there would still be visitors down there, with their accoutrements of blowing sweet papers and transistor radios. Rychester would not be her own again until the last of them had gone.

Leaving Tom to return to the school and tidy his desk, she made her way back through the park, the uphill walk tugging at the muscles behind her knees and reminding her that she was very tired. Cavendish Road awaited her return with smug complacency, its tall narrow houses neatly spaced out like a row of wallflowers waiting to be asked to dance. She turned into her own gateway. From the back garden she caught the sound of voices and could see Eva rhythmically pushing Lucy on the swing. On an impulse she turned and ran lightly up the iron staircase leading to Mrs. Bannerman's flat, breaking the unspoken taboo against "dropping in."

"Celia dear!"

"I've had rather a boozy lunch with Tom and now have a splitting headache and can't face my children! Can I claim sanctuary for an hour or so?"

"But of course, dear. Come in and I'll put the kettle on."

Incredible to remember that this gracious spacious flat had once been the attic floor of her own house. Walnut furniture gleamed richly, the silver teapot glinted. Tea with Mother was always so pleasant and relaxing. No hurried grabbing of pottery mugs but the full ritual of fragile bone china and sugar tongs. Even on this unexpected visit there was the usual plate of tiny, freshly baked cakes.

"That's better." Celia leant back in the comfortable chintz-covered chair and closed her eyes.

"I saw Lucy in the garden from the kitchen window." A pause. "I hope you did the right thing, dear, in allowing Eva to come."

Celia smiled wryly without opening her eyes. "You sound rather doubtful."

"Well, dear, as you know, I never interfere, but I should consider the matter very carefully before you become too committed. I was intending to have a word with Tom about it the next time I saw him alone. She strikes me as a very *odd* young woman. Did you notice how she kept staring at that nice Mr. Todd yesterday? I was positively embarrassed for him!"

"I don't think you need have worried on his account," Celia returned drily.

"I can't think she's a very good influence on the children."

"Oh Mother, really! It amazes me how Eva manages to excite such antipathy. After all, she doesn't *do* anything. She's completely negative. All right, granted she may have stared at Lucas Todd, but so, quite frankly, did everyone else."

"I realize, of course," Edith Bannerman said a little stiffly, "that she's your stepsister, but even so I feel you owe your first consideration to your immediate family."

"That's what Angie said, which is why we agreed to see how we got on with Eva. But we must give her a chance. She's only been here three days."

"All right, dear, you know best, of course. About Mr. Todd, though. What a charming young man he is, and so talented, Tom was saying."

"Yes."

"So fortunate to have found him, just in the nick of time."

"Yes."

"I'm sorry, dear, would you rather I kept quiet?"

Celia opened her eyes guiltily. "No, *I'm* sorry. I was being rude. It's just that all I've heard today is 'Lucas Todd' and I'm rather tired of the subject."

"You did say you had a headache, though. I'll fetch my crocheting and just sit quietly. Shall I put on some pleasant, soothing music for you?"

"No! Thank you," Celia added more quietly, aware of the older woman's startled glance. She stood up reluctantly. "I'm being boorish and abusing your hospitality. I'll come back, if I may, when I'm in a better frame of mind."

"I'm afraid I haven't been of much help."

"Of course you have. You always calm me down, and it was a delicious cup of tea, as always."

That night, Celia again dreamed of Lucas Todd. At least, she assumed it was he. He was in the likeness of the god Pan, goat-legged and sylvan, playing compelling music for her on his pipes. There was a magic circle in the grass at his feet and misty indistinct figures moved round it in a slow, drugged kind of dance. It was a disturbing dream, for all its apparent innocuity, but then anything to do with Lucas Todd, whether dream or reality, was bound to be disturbing, if not actually dangerous. She realized it, she accepted it, but how could she escape it? She lay in the darkness, the dream still spreading its tendrils about her, and her mind echoed with the strains of Pan's pipe mingled with the insistence of the music she had heard at school. Abruptly, with a conscious act of dismissal, she turned on her side and nestled closely against the warm, comforting expanse of Tom's back.

CHAPTER 4

ON the Tuesday morning, when the rush of departure for school was over, Celia found she was slightly apprehensive about her first day alone with Eva. Would the girl expect to be entertained like a visitor or to help around the house like a member of the family?

"I thought we might go shopping this morning," she began by way of compromise. "We could have coffee at Rawdons and perhaps look at some curtains I rather fancy for the drawing-room. Tom and I meant to go yesterday but we didn't get round to it."

"I'm afraid I can't manage this morning," Eva said in her colourless voice. "I have to go out myself."

"Oh?" Her semiquestion hung on the air and it became apparent it was going to remain unanswered. Eva unhurriedly finished her coffee and began to stack the breakfast dishes and load them into the dishwasher while Celia sat at the table watching her in silence. Then, with a vague smile, she slipped out of the room. The problem had resolved itself, but despite the relief, Celia was aware of a niggling and unreasonable feeling of resentment.

That day set the pattern for those that followed. Every morning soon after breakfast Eva let herself quietly out of the house, reappearing some three hours later without a word of

40

explanation as to where she had been, and Celia found it increasingly impossible to broach the subject. Occasionally she accompanied Celia to the shops in the afternoon, sometimes she volunteered to go alone to meet Lucy from school, but her mornings, Celia was tacitly given to understand, were her own affair.

Tom was inclined to laugh at her slightly indignant curiosity. "Well, I can tell you how she fills in some of the time at least," he commented. "She turns up at the school during junior break and does playground duty. I'm surprised Lucy never mentioned it."

Celia frowned. "So am I."

"I only found out myself by chance. Anyway, she won't be able to come once her own term starts."

That evening as she bathed Lucy, Celia remarked casually, "You didn't tell me Eva helps out at school."

The child shot her a quick glance under the thick fringe of her lashes. "You didn't ask," she replied, and Celia, dismissing all the logical objections to this irrefutable statement, helplessly let the subject drop.

"We're having a spelling test tomorrow," Lucy volunteered after a moment, sensing her mother's displeasure. "I do hope I come top this time."

"I hope so, too. It's usually Emma, isn't it, with you second. She must be a clever little girl, she seems to come top in most things."

Lucy scowled and did not reply and Celia, her mind still on Eva, lifted her out of the bath and began to pat her dry.

One morning during the following week Martin called round and was obviously disappointed not to find Eva at home. Celia was engaged in a batch of cake-making and he sat down at the kitchen table, watching her mixing and stirring in moody silence.

"Any thoughts yet on what you want to do?" she asked after a while.

"No. Mother and Father keep nagging, which doesn't help."

"You must see it's all been a great disappointment to them."

"Oh, I quite appreciate it would have been pleasant, especially for Mother, to talk about her son at Oxford!"

Celia looked at him in surprise. "That's not a very nice thing to say."

"Well, it's true, isn't it? You can't deny it. Mother's always been a snob."

She paused, resting on the wooden spoon. "Martin, what is it? What went wrong?"

"Everything. I just wasn't sure of anything any more. And because I refused to be hypocritical about it and carry on as though nothing had changed, all hell broke loose. They even sent Eva away to punish me, as though I were a naughty child."

"You're fond of her, aren't you?"

"Of course I'm fond of her! She's the only one of the whole lot of them who tried to understand how I felt."

"You talked it over with her?" The question wasn't meant as a rebuke but he took it as one, as, Celia realized, he took most things at the moment.

"Why shouldn't I? I had to sound out my doubts on someone. Mother and Father wouldn't listen and Ruth's pretty useless. She's been as prickly as a hedgehog since she failed her O's."

"And what was Eva's advice?"

"That it would be wrong to carry on with theology feeling as I do."

42

"I thought everyone had moments of doubt, even theologians?"

"Possibly, but it seems pointless to start off with them. You need some initial enthusiasm to get you going."

"Your mother said something about your going to France."

He flushed. "I thought at the time that Eva'd come with me, but when I mentioned it she wasn't keen. She starts college at the beginning of October and she says she has a lot to do." He looked at Celia challengingly as though blaming her for taking up Eva's time.

"And you don't want to go alone?"

He shook his head.

"It might help, you know, to get yourself sorted out if you could get away from everyone for a while. Including Eva," she added quietly. He stood up and walked over to the window, hands ploughed deep into his jeans pockets.

"Did the parents speak to her?" he demanded gruffly, his back to her. "Tell her to keep away from me or anything?"

Celia looked pityingly at the hunched shoulders. "Not that I know of. Why?"

"Oh, just that she's been pretty inaccessible since she came here. At home it was—different." His voice wobbled dangerously and she fought down a maternal desire to put her arms round him and comfort him.

"These things happen," she offered instead.

"But not as quickly as that! Dash it all, she was the one —" He broke off. Yes, Celia reflected, it may well have suited Eva to amuse herself with Martin, but that had been before she met Lucas Todd. Or perhaps, as Angie thought, having used her influence to ruin his career she had merely lost interest. In any case, there was no doubt in Celia's mind that

43

the enforced parting was the best thing that could have happened. It did not occur to her that this conclusion proved she was already halfway to accepting Angie's claims against the girl.

That evening Lucy was due for her first piano lesson and as the time approached for it Celia's restlessness grew. The younger children came out of school at three-thirty, so that although Tom was able to bring Kate home, Lucy had to be collected every day. Her music lesson was not until five, and Celia was grateful when Eva offered to meet her and bring her back for tea first.

Celia herself had not seen Lucas Todd in the ten days since he had played for them, but the unwelcome dreams of him continued, vivid and intrusive, and refused to be dismissed from her mind during the daytime. As she hurried through the park with Lucy clinging to her hand, she was thinking uncomfortably of the previous night's dream, when he had asked how long she intended to continue calling him "Mr. Todd." "Do you really imagine you can keep me at a safe distance simply by refusing to use my first name?" A safe distance. Was any distance safe enough from Lucas Todd?

The sky was full of scudding black clouds and a cold wind whipped round corners, marshalling small, rustling armies of advancing dry leaves. Lucy's endless chatter suddenly penetrated her attention.

"I did come top in my spelling last week, Mummy!"

"Well done, dear! So you managed to beat Emma at last!"

"Emma wasn't there." There was a certain quality in Lucy's voice that Celia did not understand. It was even more pronounced as she added inexplicably, "I knew she wouldn't be."

"You mean she wasn't well?"

"Yes."

"Had she felt ill the day before, then?"

"No."

"Then you could hardly have known she'd be away, could you?"

"She wasn't there," Lucy said deliberately, her voice vibrating with excitement, "because I *wished* her not to be."

Celia came to an abrupt halt, staring down at the child. "Whatever nonsense is this?"

"It *isn't* nonsense, Mummy! I wanted to be top so I wished Emma not to come. And she didn't, and I *was* top!"

Celia's face cleared slightly and she resumed walking. "It was pure chance, darling, that's all, but it's not very nice to wish for someone to be ill."

Lucy tugged angrily at her hand. "I did do it, I did! I shut my eyes and changed her colour. I knew it would work! Mr. Todd said so."

"Mr. Todd?" Celia stopped again, conscious of the sudden heavy pounding of her heart, and remembering with a wave almost of fear Lucy's secretiveness about Eva's visits to the school. What else had she not been told?

"When have you been speaking to Mr. Todd, Lucy?"

"I haven't!" the child said impatiently. "He wrote it in my book. Don't you remember? I asked him to write a message and he wrote 'Wishing will make it so.' And it does. I knew it did all the time, but grown-ups don't usually believe things like that."

"No," Celia said slowly, "and I'm quite sure Mr. Todd didn't mean it like that, either." Lucy started to speak again but Celia pulled her up sharply. "Now that's enough, Lucy. I don't want to hear any more about it. It was just chance and misunderstanding, but it's horrid even to hope that somebody would be ill just so you could come top of the class. It's like—cheating."

"It can't be cheating if it doesn't work," Lucy said sulkily and with undeniable logic. Celia held her hand rather more tightly than necessary as they came to the High Street and did not reply.

They crossed Water Lane in silence, passing close to the school, and continued along Smugglers' Walk until they reached Front Street. Here, with no buildings between themselves and the sea, the full force of the wind met them. Front Street was occasionally referred to as the upper promenade, since from its esplanade one had an uninterrupted view of sea and shore. On the far side an iron railing closed off the sheer drop to the promenade twenty feet below, broken at intervals by flights of steep stone steps. On the inland side there flourished a positive colony of buildings, now largely devoted to housing the transitory summer visitors. The junction with Smugglers' Walk formed a natural boundary between the cheaper boarding houses, ice cream parlours and souvenir shops to the west and the better-class hotels and houses to the east. Most of these houses, overlarge for present-day requirements, had been converted into flats and it was in one of these that Lucas Todd had his home.

"Mr. Todd said his flat was opposite some steps," Celia remarked as they turned left along Front Street. "This house is number 70 so it can't be this flight. It's probably the next lot."

A dog came hurrying toward them, nose to the ground, intent on its own business. Nothing else moved in the whole windswept street.

"Here it is, number 56." Celia stopped in front of a solid, handsome house. Glancing up, she saw Lucas Todd standing at the bay window on the first floor looking down at them. A moment later he appeared at the door and stood aside for them to enter.

"The door is always left on the latch," he explained, "but since it is your first visit I wanted to come down myself and welcome you. So, Lucy, you are all ready for your lesson?"

"Mr. Todd—" Lucy flung a defiant glance at her mother. "You did mean it, didn't you, about wishing making something happen? Mummy says you didn't."

Celia refused to meet the question in his eyes and he turned back to the child. "But of course I meant it, Lucy. Very often if you want something enough, you will get it." He smiled slightly. "Mind over matter, perhaps." He gestured Celia up the stairs ahead of him.

"Unfortunately," she said tightly over her shoulder as they followed her, "Lucy seems to have taken it as endowing her with magical powers!"

"Why, Lucy, what have you done?" His voice had quickened with an emotion she did not understand.

"I wanted to come top in spelling and Emma always comes top, so I wished her not to be there," Lucy said in a rush. They had reached the top of the stairs. Lucas Todd smiled slightly, showing them into the large, pleasant room overlooking the sea.

"It seems a sensible precaution!" he murmured.

"Mr. Todd, please, I was hoping for your support."

"But you have it, unreservedly, *Mrs. Bannerman.*" His voice faintly underlined her name. "May I ask the result of the experiment?"

"It worked!" Lucy's eyes glowed.

"And what became of the unfortunate Emma? Was she removed—ah—permanently?"

Lucy hesitated, uncertain what he meant, and Celia said quickly, "Of course not. I really must ask you not to encourage her. Frankly, your entry in her autograph book strikes me as rather an irresponsible one for a school master."

" 'Wishing will make it so'? It seems harmless enough to me. Was there not once a popular song of that title?"

"I've no idea," she said stiffly.

"Now, Lucy." He turned to the child, managing to convey that he had no more time to waste on trivialities. "Come and sit next to me on the piano stool. Your mother may pass the time by listening to us or looking through some magazines, whichever she prefers. You and I have important things to do."

Celia walked over to the bay window and stared out across the grey, heaving sea, struggling to contain her annoyance. He had deliberately undermined her authority, had sided with Lucy after she had tried to teach the child that what she had done was wrong. Behind her the slow, ponderous notes fell into the quiet room from Lucy's unaccustomed fingers, punctuated by the almost mesmeric voice of Lucas Todd, encouraging, advising, correcting.

For a while Celia listened to that low voice, never raised but always compelling, so completely without accent that it was more as though a highly educated foreigner were speaking than someone whose native tongue it was. Nor, she realized, did he use any modern abbreviations, which occasionally had the effect of making his speech sound stilted. For the first time she wondered whether his dark hair and sallow skin hinted at Spanish blood.

When she had herself under control again, she walked slowly back to the fireplace. An intricately wrought firescreen stood in front of the empty grate and along the shelf above was grouped an assortment of strange curios: little jade Buddhas, a replica of a Red Indian totem pole, some African carvings. She picked up one or two, turning them over in her hands, and her palms tingled slightly as though they had released some minute electrical current. Behind her Lucy's

48

laborious scale, always going wrong on the same note, beat remorselessly into her brain. She marvelled at the instructor's patience.

"Celia—" He raised his voice slightly and she spun round, startled to find him beside her and aware that he must have spoken before. He met her wide eyes with a smile. "Or are you going to insist on remaining Mrs. Bannerman?" The dream! she thought in confusion. "Are you still angry with me? I was hoping you might accept a glass of sherry as a peace offering and also as a reward for bearing so nobly with the noise we have been making. For anyone as musical as yourself, it must have been a refined torture indeed."

"Thank you," she stammered, aware in every nerve of the sheer magnetism of him. She heard herself add: "I wonder if, before we go, you might play, just for a few minutes? I— should like Lucy to hear you."

His eyes were locked on hers. "That is not entirely honest, I think. But if you ask me to play for *you,* I shall of course be delighted."

"For me, then," she acknowledged with dry lips.

He smiled and held out the glass of golden liquid.

"Thank you." She took it but he did not release his hold and her fingers brushed against his, as cold as she remembered them.

"My name is Lucas," he prompted gently.

"Thank you—Lucas." *Do you imagine you can keep me at a safe distance by refusing to use my first name?* No, she had never imagined that. To continue to refuse now would be to give the whole thing importance, which she dared not allow.

"Lucy, come and sit with your mother while I show you how you will one day play the piano."

The child moved away from the instrument reluctantly. "Is my lesson over, then?"

"For this week, yes, but you must practise at lunch time every day the way I showed you. I expect you to be very much better the next time you come."

Lucy wriggled into position beside Celia and Lucas began to play. This time there was no restlessness, no agony of discomfort. She had asked him to play for her and the music was a reward, not a punishment. Dimly she understood this without being aware that she did. Once again her most cherished desires were paraded tantalizingly before her, and on a wave of sublime euphoria she knew she could achieve them. Beside her Lucy sat unnaturally still. Her face had a closed look and her head was held slightly on one side, but her eyes never left the man at the piano.

With a crash of chords the playing stopped and as its last echoes died away Celia had to force herself to struggle back to the banality of everyday existence. Fumblingly she reached down for her handbag and as she did so, her hand knocked against a small occasional table she had not noticed before, causing it to rock and sending an ashtray skidding toward the edge. With returning coordination she caught it and exclaimed in surprise.

"What is it, Celia?"

"It's—I—we have an ashtray exactly like this one."

So exactly like it that the same hairline crack ran along one edge where the infant Kate had banged it with a wooden brick.

"You mean it is yours?"

"It can't be."

"Could Eva perhaps have brought it, in a mistaken gesture of generosity?"

"Eva?" She stared at him blankly.

"She comes here each day to clean and cook. I thought you knew."

50

Celia's mind groped hazily to make sense of what he was saying. "Eva comes here?"

"There is no cause for misgivings," he said ironically. "I am not here myself at the time. It is during school hours. Nor did I ask her to come. It is a kind thought, no doubt, but unnecessary. I am well able to look after myself."

"But if you're not here, how does she get in?"

"I never lock my door, Celia. I told you that."

"And you never see her?"

"Never." He took her hand and closed it round the ashtray. "Please take it, with my apologies. I had no idea it was not hers to give."

"You mean she's left other things?"

He shrugged, losing interest in the conversation. "From time to time. Flowers, occasionally a book."

"But if you never see her, how do you thank her for them?"

He glanced at her in genuine surprise. "I do not thank her. For the most part her gifts are of no interest to me. I do not care for flowers. They drop their petals and expect to be cared for by right, in return for their beauty."

"Then what do you do with them?"

"I throw them away," he answered calmly.

"And the books?" she asked after a moment.

"If they are of interest I glance at them."

They had both forgotten Lucy but now she spoke, in a taut, breathless little voice. "Mr. Todd, will I really be able to play like that one day?"

The rather hard line which his mouth had taken during Celia's implied criticism eased. "But of course, if you wish hard enough." His eyes, bland and implacable, rested on Celia.

"Come along, Lucy, Daddy will be wondering where we

51

are." Gravely and in silence Lucas Todd escorted them back down the stairs and pulled open the door. The cold rush of air caught their breath and tossed it away. "Thank you for the lesson," she said formally. He inclined his head, waited until they were on the pavement, and closed the door again. Celia hurried along, head down against the wind, pulling her unusually subdued daughter behind her. So Eva's morning secret was revealed after all, and it could hardly have been more unexpected. The little fool, laying herself open to his careless rebuff! What insufferable condescension: "If a book interests me, I glance at it." She imagined Eva pathetically trying to please him and pity filled her. After all, she was hardly more than a child. It was not her fault that she had been exposed to the fatal rays of Lucas Todd's charm. Celia resolved not to mention the ashtray. Its mere reappearance should be enough to discourage her from taking anything else.

CHAPTER 5

IF Eva registered the ashtray's return, she never mentioned it, nor was she any more forthcoming about her mornings spent at Front Street. To Celia's surprise Tom had not been particularly interested in her news.

"She shouldn't have taken the ashtray, obviously, but there's no harm done. As to the skivvy act, well, if she wants to, why not? I hope he appreciates his luck. No young girls came round to clean for me when I was a bachelor!"

"But he was so cold about it, not at all grateful. It humiliated me on Eva's behalf."

"I can see that masses of unwanted flowers and fruit could · become a bit of a problem. He probably doesn't want to hurt her feelings by asking her to stop."

"I doubt if Lucas Todd is even aware that people have feelings."

He frowned. "I really can't see what you've got against him. He's a fascinating chap. Everyone at school is most impressed with him, and believe me he's created quite a stir among the young female staff!"

But although Tom obviously didn't place any importance on her discovery, Celia continued to feel uneasy about it until, at the weekend, she was faced with a greater cause for concern and again seemed to be the only one to register it.

Eva had volunteered to take the children out for a walk on the Saturday afternoon and they all returned in a state of great and, Celia felt, unhealthy excitement.

Kate burst into the drawing-room without preamble. "Mummy, you'll never guess where Eva took us! To Madame Stella's! For tea!"

"Where, darling?" Celia laughingly tried to disengage herself from her daughter's enthusiastic embrace.

"To Madame Stella's. She lives in Cobble Way."

Celia's smile faded. Cobble Way ran from Water Lane to Front Street roughly parallel with Smugglers' Walk, but it was further west in a less reputable area and the pubs and cafés down at its far end were regularly subjected to police raids in search of drugs.

"Who is this Madame Stella, Kate?"

"Oh Mummy, *you* know! She's the fortune teller from the pier!"

Celia frowned. "The fortune teller? But—however did Eva know where she lived?"

"She's been there before, several times. And Mummy, she has the most *beautiful* cards! Not like ours, but all painted with men and ladies in funny costumes and—and rods and things. And she told our fortune with them!"

To Celia's annoyance Tom had not even looked up from his paper. Eva and Lucy now stood in the doorway, flushed and obviously awaiting her reaction.

"Eva, I wish you'd told me you intended to take the children to a fortune teller. I don't much care for that kind of thing."

Eva's lips tightened but before she could reply Lucy rushed to her defense. "But Mummy, Madame Stella's a *friend* of Eva's! She gave us plum cake and funny little iced biscuits in all different shapes."

54

"How long have you known this woman?" Celia demanded of Eva.

"About a year. I met her soon after I came to Rychester."

"Do you see much of her?"

"It depends. Sometimes we go for weeks without meeting." She hesitated. "She's fond of children, you know. She didn't say or do anything to frighten them."

"I just don't like their heads being stuffed with superstitious nonsense, that's all."

"Mummy—" Lucy left Eva to come and stand beside her mother, eyes glowing with excitement. "Do you know what she did? She bowed to me! Just as if I was a princess! Wasn't that funny?"

Celia glanced helplessly at Tom's newspaper. "Very, dear. Now go and take your coat off and wash your hands for tea. You too, Kate. Eva—"

Reluctantly the girl came into the room as the children left it. "Why did that woman bow to Lucy? It seems a curious thing to do."

Eva said quietly, "It was in recognition of her powers."

"Her *powers*?" Celia repeated sharply.

"Yes, she's a genuine sensitive. You know, of course, that she can see auras. She—"

Something like panic blocked Celia's throat. "Tom!" she interrupted. "Will you please show a little interest in all this!"

He folded his paper resignedly. "No need to shout, dear. I could hardly help hearing."

"Then give me some support. I won't have Lucy given all these weird ideas. It's—macabre, strange women bowing to her."

"You said yourself it's just superstititous nonsense. There's no point in getting upset about it."

"But of course I'm upset! She hasn't any powers. It's all so ridiculous."

Eva said flatly, "I'm sorry. It didn't occur to me that you'd mind."

"It's all right, Eva," Tom put in quietly. "Don't worry about it, but next time you go to see that woman, make sure you leave the children at home."

She nodded and flashed him a look of gratitude. When she had left the room Celia said accusingly, "You weren't much help."

"What did you want me to do, for Pete's sake? Wield the cane? The girl said she was sorry."

"But it's all so horrible." Her voice shook. "Lucy has not got 'powers,' whatever that means, and I won't have her frightened."

"She didn't seem frightened in the least," Tom interposed mildly. "In fact, exhilarated was the word that came to my mind."

In Celia's head Lucy's voice said positively: "I changed her colour! I knew it would work!"

"And do stop picking at your finger. You'll make it bleed."

She let her hand fall abruptly, remembering Lucas Todd. He too seemed to have sensed something in Lucy. Despite his profession, he was not one to put himself out for children— Kate he had virtually ignored—and it was surely too soon to detect any latent musical talent. At least, she told herself with overwhelming thankfulness, she was utterly convinced that he was no physical danger to the child. Disturbing though she herself found him, she knew intuitively that sexually he was cold and withdrawn. Yet the fact remained that his interest in Lucy was intense and undeniable. Grimly she wished she knew the cause of it.

Tom's voice broke into her uncomfortable thoughts.

56

"Are we having the usual celebration next weekend?"

"For your birthday? Of course."

"I saw Alan this morning—we had the school medicals—and I mentioned that you'd probably be getting in touch with him." Which meant planning another large meal, she thought resignedly, but at least there was no worry this time about the numbers totalling thirteen. There would be no question of—

"Lucas will be coming, of course."

She turned to him quickly. "Why? It's always a family party."

"Because," Tom replied with heavy patience, "I want him to. I like the chap and so does everyone else except you. You know, if you're not careful I'll begin to think you're having Freudian fancies about him!"

Celia's face flamed. "That's a disgusting thing to say. You know—"

"Well, well! 'Methinks the lady doth protest too much!' He's a damned attractive fellow, even I can see that." He gave a short laugh. "Relax, honey, I was only pulling your leg."

"I don't think it's very funny."

"Obviously. Then forget it." He picked up the paper again. Celia felt uncomfortably that there was still a barrier between them and this was unusual enough for the fact to depress her.

Since Tom had insisted, therefore, Lucas was included on the invitation list and the knowledge that he was again coming to the house filled her with a mixture of dread and restless excitement.

In the meantime, two days before the party, Lucy's second piano lesson was due. Celia was actually preparing to take her when quite suddenly she knew she couldn't. It was enough that she would be forced to spend Friday evening in his company. Two exposures to him so close together could be as lethal as an overdose of radiation. She ran downstairs and found Lucy impatiently awaiting her in the hall.

"Where's Eva?"

"I'm here." The girl appeared at the study door.

"Would you mind taking Lucy for her lesson this evening? I've suddenly developed a headache and I still have the evening meal to prepare."

Again that flash of exultation crossed her face which Celia had noticed the first time Lucas Todd's name was mentioned. And that, she thought suddenly, was before she had even met him—wasn't it?

"Now, you mean? Take her now?"

Already Celia was regretting her impulse. If Lucy was subjected simultaneously to both Eva and Lucas, with no one to help her—But the two of them, hands clasped, were already running down the path.

Twenty minutes later, Celia's white lie became an agonizing reality. Her head began to throb unbearably, her mouth went dry and she ached all over. It was as well, she reflected ruefully, searching for aspirins with a hand to her head, that she had decided against taking Lucy. The strumming piano would have been excruciating indeed. Faint and limp she crept up to her bedroom, drew the curtains and lay down. After a while the worst of the pain passed and she was able shakily to get up again and make her way downstairs.

"Mr. Todd said I played well today," Lucy reported with satisfaction on her return. "I think he was cross you didn't come, though."

"Didn't Eva explain that I had a headache?" Celia asked faintly.

"Yes, but I don't think he believed her. He smiled in a tight, funny way and said, 'A headache, has she? We'll have to see about that.' He told me to start my scales and stood very still looking out of the window for a minute or two and then he came back and we started the lesson."

Celia's fingers were like icicles in her lap. God help her, she was within inches of believing he had sent that agonizing pain to punish her as he had the minor irritations when, against her will, she first heard him play. It was the spiteful retaliation of a man unaccustomed to being resisted. But what kind of a man had the power, let alone the desire, to inflict such drastic revenge? She shivered and looked up to find Eva's eyes thoughtfully on her. Encountering hers, they immediately dropped again, but in that instant's held gaze Celia had read an odd mixture of contempt and satisfaction. Eva and Lucas. Again, for no apparent reason, her brain bracketed them together. Perhaps it was simply because she felt less than comfortable with both of them. Even more positively—and this was ludicrous—she felt threatened.

Tom's birthday was a day of sheeting rain and strong winds, with gusts of hail flung against the windows and a steady downward stream of sodden leaves. At breakfast the children presented him with their gifts: Kate's a box of hand-kerchiefs, Lucy's a bookmark painstakingly handmade. They had finished breakfast and were ready to leave for school when Eva at last appeared and handed Tom a package. He opened it hurriedly, conscious of the time, to reveal to his astonishment a beautifully produced book on ceramics. In the first shock of surprise at the sumptuousness of the gift, Celia remembered his remarking a few weeks ago that he was becoming interested in the subject.

"Eva," he stammered now, clearly taken aback, "you really shouldn't have spent so much. It's a fabulous present. I don't know what to say."

"I'm glad you like it," she answered demurely. "Happy

birthday, Tom." He bent down to kiss her as he had the children, but whether by accident or design she turned her head slightly, with the result that his kiss landed on her mouth. He withdrew quickly, a dark flush spreading over his face, and with a muttered "See you later, dear," hurriedly shepherded his daughters out of the room. Silently, with a minute smile hovering on her lips, Eva joined Celia at the breakfast table.

When the meal was over, Celia took the large sponge cake she had made out of the tin and prepared to decorate it. Traditionally Tom's birthday celebration took the form of a tea-party in which the children could join.

"I'll do that for you," Eva offered unexpectedly. Celia paused, oddly reluctant to hand over what had always been her own special task. Perhaps the girl was trying to make up for the episode of the kiss, she thought, and answered, "If you're sure you have time? Aren't you going out this morning?"

"Yes, but this won't take long. You can make a start on something else."

Sure enough it was barely half an hour later that Eva called her back to see the finished effect. Whatever Celia had expected, it was not this. The cake had been decorated with almost professional expertise, cleverly achieving the effect of basketwork with the icing intricately interwoven.

"Eva, it's beautiful!" Generously Celia bit back her dismay at the only too obvious superiority of Eva's efforts over her own. "I'd no idea this was one of your accomplishments! You must show me how you do it some time." Eva accepted the praise as impassively as she did everything and went to get ready for her usual morning outing. Celia watched her go with mixed feelings.

When Lucas arrived with the others that evening, Celia

was curious to see how he and Eva would behave toward each other after several weeks of regular if one-sided contact. It was obvious from the first that his own attitude hadn't changed in any way. He didn't spare a single glance for the girl, but Eva's fixation on him had deepened to such an extent that Celia was almost alarmed. She remarked on it to Tom when he came to the kitchen to help her carry through the tea things.

"Oh for heaven's sake, not that again! I've told you, the girls at school are exactly the same. He's a good-looking chap, it's natural enough."

"But that's just the point, Tom," she insisted in a low voice. "With Eva it's decidedly unnatural. It isn't normal hero-worship. In fact, it's more like worship without the 'hero.' "

"I really can't think why you get so worked up about it. She won't come to any harm. It would be quite different if he was chasing her. Now get a move on, for goodness sake. Surely that kettle must be boiling."

When they reached the dining-room, it was to find that the children had already shown the visitors through and Lucas Todd had taken up his previous place on Celia's right. She had no option but to sit beside him.

As was to be expected, the exquisite cake was the center of admiration and Celia had repeatedly to pass the congratulations she received over to Eva, who accepted them all smugly with lowered eyes. The only dissenting voice was Kate's. "But it looks too good to eat! I like Mummy's decorations best. They're all soft and squidgy when you bite into them." Down the table Celia sent her a look of heartfelt gratitude.

"No more headaches?" Lucas enquired of her later as they waited for Tom to cut the cake.

"No, thank you."

"It was unfortunate that you missed Lucy's lesson. She has made what I feel we could justifiably call startling progress in one week."

"I'm glad to hear it." She glanced down the length of the table at Tom and noticed that his eyes were on Eva. Perhaps after all he would come to admit there was something unhealthy about the girl's obsession with Lucas. With luck it might all fizzle out of its own accord when she returned to college in a week's time. Automatically Celia's attention switched to Martin, sullen and morose beside Lucy. He had not eaten much and was now pushing the obligatory piece of cake to the side of his plate. She might have one ally after all in her dislike of Lucas Todd.

The meal was followed, as always, by a few rounds of *Consequences,* to the children's squealing delight. Then, again as always, they were dispatched reluctantly to bed, Tom moved to the drinks cabinet, and the adults settled down for an enjoyable evening.

"Kate was regaling me during tea with the eccentricities of the Robin Hood film she'd seen," Mrs. Bannerman remarked with a smile. "I must admit I find the thought of King John sucking his thumb somewhat nauseating!"

"Hands off good old English tradition, eh Mother?" Tom teased her.

"Walt Disney isn't the only one to probe the Robin Hood legend," Alan remarked ruefully. "I remember reading somewhere that they were in reality a coven of witches!"

"What nonsense!" Angie declared stoutly. "I refuse to believe it! If you ask me, it's just cashing in on this current mania for the supernatural."

"I'm not so sure. From what I remember there was quite a lot of talk in the stories about shooting arrows through

62

garlands, and that's a recognized witch symbol. And apparently the Major Oak in Sherwood Forest, where Robin used to meet Maid Marian, is still used as the meeting place for a coven."

"Still?" Melanie echoed incredulously, making one of her rare contributions to the conversation. "You're surely not trying to tell us that there are still witches today? *Here?* In *England?*"

"Most certainly there are," Alan declared positively. "It's far more prevalent than most people realize, not to mention safer than it has been for the last six hundred years, since the Witchcraft Acts were repealed."

"You seem to know a lot about it," Tom commented drily. "You haven't by any chance a cosy little coven yourself, have you?"

Alan laughed. "My interest is purely academic, I assure you, but as a medical man I have to keep up with all this. Heaven knows what we'll be asked to accept next. Acupuncture, hypnotic healing—any of these practices would have got you burned at the stake a couple of centuries ago. Now as things are going you'll probably soon be able to get them on the National Health!"

"But surely," Melanie persisted, "in this scientific age people don't really believe in all that mumbo jumbo?"

"My dear girl, rather to its embarrassment this scientific age is having to admit more and more that 'mumbo jumbo' as you call it is not nearly as ridiculous—or as harmless—as we'd all supposed."

"I imagine you're referring to voodoo and the death spells we hear about from time to time?" Michael suggested. "Surely it's just that primitive people are so credulous that they only have to be convinced a spell has been put on them for them conveniently to sicken and die."

"Autosuggestion, you mean? No, Mike, it's not quite as simple as that. That was what we told ourselves for long enough, I grant you, but recent work on telepathy—another example of vindicated mumbo jumbo—has proved that it is actually possible to transmit emotions and physical illness telepathically. All that's needed is sufficient concentration, and that can be acquired by adjusting the rhythm of the sender's brainwaves."

"Holy Moses, is it possible to do that consciously?"

"Oh yes. Mind you, it's still rare enough to be considered abnormal but it's certainly not supernatural. It's done in much the same way that mediums achieve a state of trance."

Almost fearfully, Celia glanced at the rapt faces of Eva and Lucas Todd. They were at opposite sides of the room, but the expression on their faces was identical—an intense, guarded excitement. So it was possible for Lucas to have transmitted the sensations with which she had already credited him, and not after all by supernatural so much as hypernormal means.

"What about clairvoyance and second sight?" Ruth demanded eagerly. "Is there some scientific explanation of them too, Uncle?" Before he could reply she turned to Eva. "By the way, Kate said you'd been to Madame Stella again. Did she have anything of interest?"

"Who in heaven's name is Madame Stella?" Angie demanded. "This conversation is rapidly getting beyond me!"

"You know, Mum, the rather creepy fortune teller from the pier. I went along with Eva once or twice, soon after she came to live with us."

"And what did she tell you?" Martin asked with interest.

There was a brief pause. "Good grief!" Ruth said slowly. "I'd forgotten all about it, but she said something about failing my exams. I just dismissed it and never thought about it again." She turned to Alan. "Does that mean I was preconditioned, Uncle?"

"If you're trying to tell us it wasn't your fault," her father put in drily, "it just won't wash!"

"It's an interesting point, though, Dad." Martin was showing the first sign of animation his family had seen in him for months. "Which is cause and which effect? I mean, did Ruth subconsciously fail because she'd been told she would, or would she have done anyway?"

"Search me. What I don't understand is whyever Eva went to see the woman in the first place."

Everyone looked at the girl and a pale flush suffused her face. Since a reply to the indirect question seemed to be expected, she said after a moment, "I went originally because I wanted to learn to read the Tarot."

"The what?"

"The Tarot cards. It's a very ancient form of fortune telling."

"And did she teach you?" Angie demanded suspiciously.

"Yes. Actually my mother started to, but she died before she could tell me everything. I wanted to fill in the gaps and check a few points."

"Irenka used to read these cards?" Alan asked with interest.

"Yes, it's been in the family for generations. Hungarian gypsies have sometimes been credited with inventing them, but actually the Tarot was in existence long before the gypsies reached Europe."

"So you can tell fortunes yourself now?" Ruth asked excitedly. "Jolly good, it will save me twenty pence! Have you any of these special cards of your own?"

For a second Eva glanced at Lucas Todd, but as always

he was not looking at her. His eyes were on Ruth's bright, eager face and there was a slight smile on his lips.

"I have, yes."

"Will you tell my fortune then? Now?"

Eva said slowly, "It takes rather a long time to do it properly, Ruth. Also, certain times are more—propitious—than others, times when signs can be more easily interpreted. One of the best, of course, is birthdays." She paused and her eyes went to Tom who, like the others, was watching her with acute attention. As their eyes met it seemed to Celia that his colour deepened slightly and she wondered with a touch of affectionate exasperation whether he was remembering the unintentional kiss that morning.

Eva said softly, "Would you like me to give you a birthday reading, Tom?"

He moved a little uncomfortably. "I'm not at all sure that I would!"

"Then do me!" Ruth pleaded.

"Oh come on, Tom, there's nothing to worry about!" Angie urged him, obviously reluctant for her daughter to take part in anything so dubious.

"I didn't realize quite what I was starting when I mentioned Robin Hood!" Mrs. Bannerman remarked with a rather uncertain laugh.

"Shall I, Tom?" Eva repeated. At last he nodded. She went quietly from the room and a few minutes later returned with a small wooden box.

"Put up the card table, Martin," Michael instructed, and a moment later Eva and Tom were seated opposite each other across the green baize while the rest of them crowded round. Eva opened the box and took out a packet wrapped in purple silk. This she laid on the table and opened it carefully to reveal a pack of large, highly coloured cards. Ruth put out an inquisitive hand but Eva moved swiftly to intercept it.

"No—please. The cards must never be handled casually. They should only be touched by the reader and the querient —the person whose destiny is being foretold."

Melanie said to no one in particular, "She really believes in it, doesn't she?" No one replied, but a faint ripple of unease moved over them. Eva had spread the purple silk over the entire surface of the table and was engaged in shuffling the cards, occasionally turning one from top to bottom as she did so. She looked across at Tom.

"Which spread would you like? There's one for the year ahead, or one to answer a specific question, or—"

"Oh, just a general one," Tom muttered, and again Celia was aware of his heightened colour. "Certainly not the year ahead—I'd rather not know!"

She handed him the pack. "Now you shuffle as I did, reversing some of the cards as you go along. I'll do the Nine Card Spread, then. It relates to past, present and future."

Clumsily Tom began to shuffle the large cards. "I'm beginning to regret letting you all talk me into this!"

"I'll take it now." Eva's voice was quiet and authoritative. Holding the pack face downwards, she began to lay one card after another on the silk-covered table in a series of rows. The others moved closer to watch. Only Lucas Todd, with the half-smile still on his lips, remained in his former place.

"Don't you believe in the Tarot, Mr. Todd?" Ruth asked him. He shrugged slightly.

"My dear, I have seen so many. My main interest is in the interpretation and I can hear that quite well from here."

Eva gave no sign of having heard the exchange. Her entire concentration was focused on the table in front of her and the man who sat unmoving opposite. She reached out and turned a card face up.

"The King of Swords," she said softly. "As I expected. This first card indicates your present circumstances. It shows that you are in a position of authority, that you're intelligent and are a good organizer."

"The King of Swords? He looks more like Old King Cole to me," Tom remarked with the facetiousness of relief. "Okay, carry on. I hope they're all like that!"

"The four of Cups. This tells us that your emotional happiness is now at a peak. You are beginning to realize that there is nothing further you can achieve and dissatisfaction is beginning to creep in. You're wondering, in fact, where you go from here."

Celia glanced quickly at Tom and saw him bite his lip. This time he offered no comment. With a rhythmic, almost mechanical gesture, Eva turned the next card, which was upside down. "The Ace of Batons reversed," she continued. "Not a very lucky card, I'm afraid. It shows pride and greed and an over confidence that could end in destruction."

Nobody spoke, nobody met anyone else's eyes. In the almost oppressive silence Eva's soft, remorseless voice went on. "The nine of Batons, again reversed. This is the card which gives the background to your present conditions. It shows you have been obstinate in the past and refused to compromise. With a more flexible attitude you might not have been brought to the present moment of decision."

Tom stirred uneasily. "I'm not so sure I like all these home truths. You make it sound so plausible."

Eva waited politely for him to finish speaking, then silently proceeded to the next card, this one in a row by itself. "Seven of coins." She smiled very slightly. "Well, at least there's a faint ray of hope here. Good fortune is still possible, but only if you pull yourself together. At the moment you are wasting efforts which you made in the past."

Celia bent forward, wishing that this sinister party game would end. She could see that the general negative nature of the reading was having its effect. Tom's mouth had rather a set look to it. Almost hypnotized herself, she stared down at the newly upturned card, reversed again and therefore facing her. It depicted a tall building toppling sideways with two figures falling from it, and her mind flew superstitiously to the children. But Eva was continuing calmly: "The Tower reversed. This card is one of the Major Arcana and therefore very important. I'm afraid it bears out the overall tone of the others. Foundations are crumbling, leaving you insecure and without confidence. And here's the same thing yet again— the five of Swords. Before you can look for success you'll have to face defeat and swallow your pride."

"All right," Tom muttered under his breath. "You've made your point. I'm in for a hard time. It scarcely seems worth bothering with the last two."

"Five of Batons," Eva continued inexorably. "A difficult fight lies ahead but it can be overcome by quick thinking and immediate action. I don't think I've ever had such a consistent reading before. And here's the last one." Her hand flicked over the final anonymous card and Celia gave a little cry. There in front of her was the Pan-like figure she had in her dream identified with Lucas, horned, goat-legged, crouching on a stone.

"The Devil," Eva said, her voice scarcely above a whisper. "This card signifies that there are hidden forces at work. There is a danger of corruption and emotional upheaval."

Tom pushed back his chair. "Well, thanks very much. I don't mind telling you that's the last time I'll submit to anything like that. Ye gods, what a prospect! It's just as well

I don't believe it." His eyes went challengingly round the circle of faces. His only answer was an occasional strained smile.

Celia turned from the shrouded table to meet the steady gaze of Lucas Todd. Did he know that he had figured in her dreams ever since they had met, not only as Pan but also as his equally disturbing self? Beside her, Ruth said under her breath, "Poor Uncle looks rather shattered. I do think she might have put in *something* on the credit side."

"She couldn't if there was nothing there," Celia answered dully. Michael and Martin were folding up the card table and Eva, the cards safely shut away again in their box, murmured something inaudible and left the room. It occurred to Celia that no one had thanked her for the reading. Standing next to Alan, Tom watched her go, and on his face was an expression of resigned, baffled acceptance. Despite his denial, Celia knew with a heavy heart that he had accepted the entire interpretation. It remained to be seen what steps he would take to overcome it.

CHAPTER 6

AFTERWARDS, Celia dated the change in Tom from that evening. At the time, however, she was too disturbed herself to notice anything, for on the night of the birthday party she had her most vivid dream yet of Lucas Todd—her most vivid and her most disturbing. It seemed that they were at opposite ends of a large bare room. From where she stood his figure was foreshortened, oddly puppet-like and yet full of a menacing magnetism.

Slowly, and desperately against her will, she felt herself being compelled toward him. Frantically she reached back, clawing for some fingerhold on the wall behind her, but it was as smooth as glass. Helplessly, one foot dragging after the other, she slowly and jerkily moved across the vast expanse of empty floor toward him. And as she approached his figure became more and more attenuated, growing alarmingly in height as it diminished in width, like a shadow stretching up the wall behind him.

At last she reached him, and he was suddenly on her level, his face only inches away from hers, his cold, gold-tinted eyes gazing deep into her own. And still the powerful magnetism went on drawing her closer, so that she reached up and kissed him on the mouth. At the contact a deep chill ran shudderingly through her and she clasped both hands to her lips as though they were frostbitten. He smiled mockingly down at her and said, "Why do you continually fight me, Celia? You must know I shall win in the end."

Still in the dream she began to weep, soundlessly and despairingly and for a time he watched her without interest. Then he reached out and plucked a dark red rose from a bush which, as is the way of dreams, had unaccountably sprung up beside him. He leant forward and tucked the flower into the bodice of her dress, but a sharp thorn drove into her flesh and when she looked down the passage of the stem had left a beaded red line on her skin.

She woke with a jerk and stared wild-eyed at the lightening room. Yet even the solid familiarity of her surroundings was not enough to comfort her. Admittedly she was no longer in the vast bare hall, but Lucas Todd came to this house and though the dream was gone, the danger implicit in it was still very much with her.

Gradually her breathing quietened and she lay drained, deliberately expunging the dream from her mind. Beside her, Tom tossed and turned restlessly. Would he blame Eva for the future she had outlined for him the previous evening? Sadly, Celia acknowledged to herself that her own attitude toward the girl had changed drastically since she came to the house. Perhaps it had been unwise to dismiss Angie's experiences out of hand. Yet, after all, what had she done? As Angie said, it was hard to pinpoint anything. Apart from the minor episode of the ashtray there was no concrete accusation, merely vague instances of disquiet: her obsession over Lucas Todd and her reticence about going to his flat, the visit with the children to the fortune teller. She could hardly return the girl summarily to Angie on the grounds that there was nothing remaining of the beloved little stepsister in the secretive, self-effacing Eva of today.

72

It was as they were dressing later that Tom's voice cut into her musings. "Whatever have you been doing to yourself?"

She turned enquiringly and, following his gesture, glanced down. Across the top of her breast ran a deep, diagonal scratch.

Briefly she wondered if she was going to faint, for all the usual morning noises—a car in the road outside, Kate's radio —came and went in undulating waves, unable to penetrate her own innate silence.

"What are you looking like that for?" Tom demanded in amused exasperation. "There doesn't seem much likelihood of bleeding to death!"

"I—was just surprised," she stammered at last. "I suppose I must have done it in my sleep." As, indeed, she must, and possibly the self-inflicted pain had woven itself into her dream in the form of the rose-thorn with which Lucas had pierced her flesh.

But rationalize it as she would, for as long as the scratch remained on her skin it served as a potent reminder of Lucas Todd and the chill of his lips when, in her dream, she had attempted to kiss him.

"Lucy's piano playing is improving quite incredibly," Tom remarked the following week. "I went along to the music wing today during her practice. Have you heard her lately?"

"No, not since her first lesson, which was somewhat disastrous."

"There's nothing disastrous about it now, believe me. Lucas must be the most fantastic teacher. Isn't it this evening she goes? You'll hardly believe the difference in her."

Celia opened her mouth to say she would not be taking Lucy to her lesson, but closed it again. After all, she had a limited choice. Either she risked that appalling headache with which he had punished her defection last time or, with the dream still raw in her mind, she must submit once more to whatever influence he chose to level against her.

But, like the last time she had built up a panic defense against him, her apprehension was needless. Lucas was charming and courteous—and Lucy played brilliantly. Celia could scarcely believe it was her daughter sitting confidently on the stool, her hands speeding lightly over the keys, involved in some quite complicated finger movement. With less pleasure, though, she was acutely and uncomfortably aware of the strong bond which had built up between the man and the child. Their attention was centered wholly on each other, and Celia, the sole object of his interest in her fraught, egotistical dreams, was to her shame curiously deflated. "Freudian fancies" Tom had called them—and they were. Her cheeks flamed as she remembered again her dream-temerity in reaching to kiss him, and in that moment he looked across at her smilingly, anticipating her delight in Lucy's playing and adding considerably to her confusion.

"Well, Celia, are you proud of your daughter?" he enquired when, with a final chord, Lucy's hands dropped to her lap.

"It's—phenomenal." It was ungracious, but she found herself wishing that Lucy had been much less proficient, had made only the small amount of progress which under normal conditions could have been expected in so short a time. Instinctively she formed a mental blockage against defining "normal conditions."

"She has obviously inherited your own talent," he said smoothly, his golden eyes blandly refuting her unspoken reservations. "All she needed was the stimulus to start playing and she was away."

Uncomfortably Celia remembered the Lucy of only a fort-

74

night ago who had asked in awe, "Will I really be able to play like that?" and his reply: "If you wish hard enough." The needle-prick of apprehension jabbed her again. With an effort she rose to her feet.

"Come along, dear, supper will be ready and we've taken up enough of Mr. Todd's time." He made no attempt to detain them.

On the way home Celia made an effort to overcome her persistent uneasiness. "You really played wonderfully well this evening, darling. You must have been practising very hard to have learned so quickly."

Lucy bent to retrieve a conker, satin smooth, from the debris of leaves at the side of the path. "No I haven't. I hate practising—it's so boring."

"But Daddy told me himself that he heard you."

Lucy giggled. "He told me he was coming and I thought he'd be cross if I wasn't there. He'd never believe that it's much easier just to wish."

"I should think not," Celia said sharply. "Wishing by itself is no good."

"Mr. Todd helps, of course," the child agreed.

She gave a little laugh. "Helps? I should think he does! He—"

But Lucy was continuing, "It's queer really, Mummy. His eyes come into mine and I feel sort of funny and then very strong, and I know I can do anything I want."

Celia jerked to a halt, the suddenness of her stop spinning the child round to face her. "What are you talking about? What do you mean, his eyes come into yours?" The incipient hysteria was discernible in her voice.

Lucy frowned. "They just do, that's all." She tugged at her hand. "Don't hold me so tightly, Mummy. You're hurting."

"Lucy—" Celia strove to keep her voice steady. "Darling,

you mustn't take it seriously, you know, all this nonsense about wishing for things. Mr. Todd is only teasing you. He doesn't expect you to believe it."

"He *does* mean it," Lucy said stubbornly. "He wrote it in my book. He thinks I'm very clever. Not many people realize getting things is so easy."

"But at your first lesson he told you you must practise," Celia persisted, with something like desperation. "I heard him myself."

Lucy said patiently, "But he meant practise *wishing,* not the piano."

Celia was looking at her with a helpless feeling of fear. This child with her closed, obstinate face was the one she had loved and looked after for the last six years. But she was also the one old Madame whatever-her-name-was had bowed to in recognition of her "powers." "She's a true sensitive," Eva had said. "She sees auras." What in hell was an aura?

A chill scarf of wind trailed over them and Lucy shivered. "What are we waiting for, Mummy? I'm cold. Let's go home."

Responding to the tug on her hand, Celia began to walk again. "Darling, you know that game of colours that you play?"

"It's not—"

"What colour did Mr. Todd have round him today?"

Lucy said slowly, "He didn't have a colour. He never has."

"But I thought you said everyone had one?" Celia seized with relief on this inconsistency. Obviously the child had forgotten some of the rules of the game she had invented.

"It's not only people, it's animals and flowers too."

"All right then," Celia humoured her. "If even animals and flowers have these coloured lights of yours, surely Mr. Todd must have one as well?"

She shook her head positively. "But he hasn't. I don't know why. I keep meaning to ask him but I always forget."

The recurring cameo of the two of them together at their first meeting came into focus in Celia's head. What was it the child had said? Something which at the time had sounded a warning without her realizing why. *It's funny your name meaning light because you haven't got one.* And Lucas had leant forward slightly, his eyes no doubt "going into hers," so that when Michael had tried to prompt her, Lucy had forgotten what she was trying to say.

With a supreme effort of will, Celia clenched her chattering teeth. Of all the far-fetched, ridiculous things! After supper she'd tell Tom what she had been imagining, making a joke of it, and their shared laughter would banish the idea for good.

But after supper Tom was tired and irritable and refused to be drawn into conversation and the uneasiness was still unexpurgated the next morning when, unannounced, Alan called and enquired if he was in time for coffee.

"Of course," Celia said gladly, "Come through with me while I make it."

"I've a number of calls round here so I thought I'd give myself fifteen minutes' break." He pulled out a chair and sat down at the kitchen table. "Unfortunately the unseasonably cold weather has meant an earlier start to flu this year. How's Tom? None of the children at school affected, I hope?"

"Not as far as I know." Celia turned from filling the kettle. "Actually, he's been rather prickly ever since Eva told his fortune."

"Poor Tom! He sounded to have a sticky time ahead!"

"What's rather surprising," Celia continued deliberately, "is that I have the impression that he believes it."

77

"Does he now? Well, Eva was very convincing, I must say. She seemed to have it all off pat."

"It *isn't* possible, is it Alan? To tell the future from a pack of cards?"

"Lord, love, don't ask me, I'm only an ordinary G.P.! I don't see how it can be, but as I said that evening, things are constantly being accepted these days that ranked as superstitions only a few years ago."

"Like Robin Hood being a warlock?" Celia suggested with a forced laugh.

"Perhaps; incidentally, Robin was one of the names for the devil in the seventeenth century."

"You don't really believe in the devil, do you, Alan?"

"Good heavens, little sister! What searching questions for eleven o'clock on a Thursday morning!"

"Well, do you?"

"I don't know. I daresay the force of evil can be personified if one accepts that the force for good is."

"Alan, I don't like Lucas Todd. I think *he's* a force for evil."

"Lucas?" He looked up in surprise as she put the coffee in front of him. "I thought he was rather a pleasant chap."

"He has some kind of hold over Lucy," she said jerkily. Her brother frowned. "How do you mean?"

"I don't know exactly. She plays the piano beautifully, for example, and she's only had three lessons."

"I'd hardly call that a force for evil! You should—"

"But she hasn't practiced at all! You know how lazy she is, she always opts for the easy way. She says he just looks at her and she knows she can do it."

"Then I wish he'd look at me sometimes and tell me what the hell I ought to do about old Mrs. Jenkins' leg!"

"*Please* be serious, Alan. It frightens me."

"Hey!" He reached out and caught her hand, gently pulling her onto the chair beside him. "What is all this? You're surely not serious about Lucas exerting some kind of evil influence?"

"Yes I am, and I can't get anyone else to see it. That's what frightens me. No one will hear a word against him. Eva looks at him as though he were some kind of god, you and Tom insist he's a 'pleasant chap' and Angie, Mother and Melanie preen every time he glances in their direction."

"But surely it's all very hypothetical. There's nothing you can *prove* against him, is there?"

"Not yet," she replied, and shivered.

"Oh Celia, come on, love, snap out of it! He's different, I'll give you that, but how boring it would be if we were all the same. I certainly don't see him as a Svengali towering over poor little Lucy, but if you do, surely all you have to do is stop her music lessons."

"Tom wouldn't hear of it."

"Well, I must say I can't blame him. You say she's making excellent progress. It does seem rather a strange reason to take her away."

"But she's so—susceptible. You know how she's always talked all this nonsense about lights and colours round people—"

"Auras? Has she really? I didn't know that."

She looked at him sharply. "That's the word Eva used, but surely it's only the rubbish mediums and people like that talk about?"

"Not any more, I'm afraid. An aura is an electrical force field round the body. It's there all right—thermographic photographs have proved it. Didn't you see that series they did in one of the colour supplements? It's even being used in advanced circles for medical diagnosis."

"However can they do that?"

"Because its colour and shape changes with a person's moods or physical condition."

"You honestly believe that?" It was horribly close to what Lucy had always maintained.

"My dear girl, it's a fact."

Celia stared at him, coldness closing over her. "Then why can Lucy see it, when we can't?"

"It doesn't mean she's a spiritualist or anything," Alan said gently. "Just as some people can hear supersonic sounds, so others can see wavelengths that most of us can't. It's tied up with the rods and cones in the eye; the rods in some people are more developed—like cats and other animals that can see in the dark—and they can detect infrared rays and so on."

She stirred her coffee reflectively. Then: "Lucy said Lucas Todd hasn't got one," she said in a flat voice.

"Hasn't got an aura? He must have."

"That's what I said, but she insisted he hadn't."

Alan put down his cup carefully. "Now that *is* interesting. I read a fascinating book once on auras. In it, a man said he used to sit and watch people passing like a lot of luminous eggs. Every now and then he'd see someone in the crowd who didn't glow, and would know that—"

"Go on." Celia's mouth was dry.

"—that without it, it couldn't be a real person."

"Couldn't—? Then what in heaven's name was it?"

Alan smiled a little and drained his cup. "If we get involved in this I'll forget all the calls I'm supposed to be making and Mrs. Taylor's baby will make its arrival without me. Seriously, though, I shouldn't take too much notice of what Lucy says. She's an imaginative child and probably doesn't see half the things she says she does."

80

"What terrifies me is that what she says she sees really exists after all. And the fortune teller—"

"Honey, I just haven't time to hear about your soothsayers. Forget it. It's a dangerous state of mind to get into, being too credulous."

For a long time after he had gone, Celia sat where he had left her, her mind going over what he had said. It was difficult to accept that Alan hadn't known about Lucy's "lights" when most of the family had always been aware of them. But of course no one had taken them seriously and if he just hadn't happened to be there when she spoke of them certainly no one would have thought them worth mentioning to him. Her mind switched abruptly to his last words, about the man who made a habit of watching auras and his conclusion when someone didn't possess one. "Not a real person."

She stood up quickly, her brain shying away from implications too stupendous to assimilate. It was imperative to find something to do, at once, something ordinary and everyday to dispel this occult dread which was beginning to take hold of her. Thankfully she remembered the clean laundry still waiting to be sorted and put away, and she almost ran upstairs to the linen cupboard. Forcing herself to close her mind to everything but the task in hand, she divided the neatly ironed garments into separate piles, the children's, Eva's, her own and Tom's. Tom had complained about a shortage of shirts in his drawer yesterday. She must check to see if any had been overlooked in the laundry basket.

With a pile of clothes in her hand, she was halfway across Eva's room before awareness of the unusual smell travelled from her nostrils to her brain. She stopped and sniffed curiously. It was tallow. Puzzled, she glanced round the room trying to locate its source. Nothing immediately suggested

81

itself. Slowly she went over to the chest of drawers and put the clothes in the top drawer as she did every week. Then, on an impulse of which she was not proud but which she didn't pause to define, she quickly opened the three lower drawers one after the other, running her hands swiftly under the neat piles of blouses, sweaters and underwear. In the far corner of the bottom drawer, hidden under layers of clothes, her fingers encountered the hard outline of a box. Slowly she pulled it out and opened the lid. It was half full of ordinary kitchen candles such as she herself kept in case of power cuts. She stood looking down at them until the sudden sound of voices near at hand made her jump guiltily and push the box back into its hiding place. As her heartbeats steadied, she realized that the voices were coming from the iron staircase which went up the side of the house just beyond Eva's window and led to Mrs. Bannerman's flat.

She heard her mother-in-law's light, pleased laugh, and then a voice which she identified instantly. "But of course. It's my pleasure, Edith."

"Edith" indeed! She moved to the side of the window and, screened by the curtain, watched the two figures descend. As they reached the ground, Lucas took the old woman's hand and tucked it under his arm. She could no longer detect the words, but they were talking animatedly as they moved out of her field of vision. For a moment she was conscious of total loneliness. Even the pleasant flat on the top floor was no longer available to her as a refuge. He had been welcome there. She could hope for no support from her mother-in-law in her solitary struggle against this man and the influence which he was slowly extending over all of them.

She turned back to close the drawer containing the candles. She couldn't imagine why they were there. Possibly Eva was afraid of the dark and ashamed that anyone should know it. If that were so, the nightlights the children used to have were considerably safer in their holders than an unsupported candle and Celia could see no candlestick or tall vase into which a candle could be stuck.

She was leaving the room when her eye fell on something which lay on the floor half hidden under the dressing table, and she bent to pick it up. It was Tom's tie pin. However—? He never wore it, anyway. Perhaps this was intended, like the ashtray, as a present for Lucas Todd. Celia was aware of anger. Obviously her leniency over the ashtray had been misconstrued and the girl felt free to steal anything she chose with impunity. She would have to be spoken to after all. Celia slipped the pin into her pocket and thankfully left the room.

When tackled that evening, Eva denied all knowledge of how the tie pin came to be in her room. She stubbornly repeated that one of the children must have borrowed and dropped it, and nothing Celia said could shake her. The confrontation finished with Eva turning and running blindly from the room, cannoning into Tom in the doorway.

"What on earth's going on now?" he demanded as she fled past him up the stairs.

Celia said tightly, "I found your tie pin in her room. Presumably she was going to take it to Lucas."

He stared down at it in the palm of her hand. "That old thing? He's welcome to it!"

"That's hardly the point, Tom. Eva had it."

"But it's completely worthless. It's not real gold, you know."

"Don't you see what I mean? She's still taking things that don't belong to her. It's a horrible feeling, having someone in the house who—"

"For Pete's sake, Celia, stop picking on the girl! You're as bad as Angie!"

Celia stared at him speechlessly.

"Lord, it's like the Middle Ages when you were liable to be hanged for stealing a loaf of bread! I won't have the girl upset like this."

"*You* won't—" Celia choked.

"No, I won't have her made to feel she's a criminal. It's too stupid for words."

"But—"

"I don't want to hear anything more about it. I'll go and see if I can soothe her down. She was nearly in tears, poor little thing."

He turned and strode from the room, leaving Celia gazing after him with blazing cheeks, her thoughts in chaos. She had been so disturbed by the threat of Lucas Todd on the fringes of their existence that she had completely overlooked Eva, safely ensconced in the heart of the family and gnawing away at its very core.

CHAPTER 7

FOR the next few days the strained atmosphere between Tom and Celia continued. Eva was her usual quiet, subdued self, but Celia was aware that her lowered lids did not prevent her from seeing everything that went on. Even the children, sensing something not quite as it should be, reacted by being difficult and bad-tempered. Lucy in particular was truculent and disobedient and it seemed to Celia that she was constantly engaged in a battle of wills with the child.

On Sunday Mrs. Bannerman came to lunch as usual, and when she was helping to clear the table after the meal, Celia remarked casually, "I saw you with Lucas Todd the other day. I didn't know you entertained gentlemen up there!"

The older woman smiled. "He came round with a sheaf of the most glorious autumn leaves. He'd heard me say at Tom's party how I love them. Wasn't it thoughtful of him? And he insisted on driving me to the shops afterwards. He was most surprised when he heard I usually have to walk."

Celia turned and looked at her in amazement. "But Mother, you know you always insist on walking! I could run you down any time you want, but—"

"Yes, well, sometimes it does seem rather a long way, especially when my leg is stiff."

"I didn't know your leg was ever stiff. Has Alan seen it?"

"Now don't fuss, dear. I only meant that it was very pleasant to have a lift for once, and he's such an attentive young man."

"All the same, I rather resent his assumption that we don't look after you."

"My dear! He never suggested any such thing!"

"But he was 'surprised' to hear we don't usually run you to the shops. If that wasn't implied criticism, I don't know what is. If it comes to that," she added before she could stop herself, "*I* was surprised to find that he called you by your first name. Even Alan and Michael don't do that."

Mrs. Bannerman flushed. "My dear Celia, it sounds almost as though you've—what's that rather curious American phrase?—'bugged' my flat. In any case, I was not aware that I was answerable to you as to whom I invite up there nor whom I allow to use my Christian name."

"Mother, I'm sorry. It was only—look, I didn't mean to make you angry." She slipped an arm contritely round the unyielding body and kissed the still averted cheek. "I'm afraid I just don't like the man. I realize I'm alone in that and it makes me a bit edgy."

"I'm sure I don't know what there is to dislike in him. In any case, he seems to like you. He was asking quite a lot of questions about you."

Celia went rigid. "What kind of questions?"

"Goodness, I don't know. What does it matter? You've nothing to hide, surely." With equanimity still so finely balanced between them, Celia did not pursue the matter.

The days followed each other with seeming uneventfulness. Even the much-discussed General Election came and went without exciting any interest. With the sudden onset of much colder weather, the family moved, as they did every winter, from the large and rather draughty drawing-room at

86

the back of the house to the smaller and much warmer study at the front. Usually Celia loved this time of the year and the switch of rooms heralded a drawing together of the family. In the long dark evenings there was no question of the children going out to play after school, and they were content to settle down after tea to watch children's television or, in the case of Kate, to read. The leather armchairs, the dark red wallpaper and brown velvet curtains wrapped Celia in a warm cocoon of changelessness and in her mental picture of the room the curtains were always drawn, the fire blazing and the table drawn up in front of it for tea.

This year, however, she had been conscious of a curious sense of holding back, of trying to keep at bay the cold, shortening days which were almost upon them, and it was not until Tom, with the irritation he was beginning to show more and more, demanded how much longer he had to freeze in the drawing-room that she reluctantly effected the changeover. For the first time she was aware of autumn as a time of dying, the end of something rather than a joyous approach to the crackling ice and roaring fires of winter.

One evening when Tom was out at an open evening, Lucy appeared in pyjamas and dressing-gown with the request for Celia to brush her hair. On the other side of the fire, Eva was sitting quietly reading. Feeling closer to the child than she had for some time, Celia deftly brushed the fall of shining hair, contentedly breathing in the pleasant scent of soap and talcum powder which lingered from bathtime an hour or so before.

"There you are, darling. Off to bed now." And as the child bent to kiss her, she added, "It's a long time since I heard you say your prayers, Lucy. You don't forget them when you go upstairs, do you?"

The child hesitated and her large grey eyes fell away from Celia's.

"You still say them, don't you dear?" Celia persisted, aware now of Eva's attention and oddly disturbed by it.

"Not always," Lucy muttered at last.

"But you should. Kneel down now and say them for me like you used to."

Lucy glanced across at Eva but the girl's eyes were on her book.

"Come along, Lucy. You're not shy of Eva, surely?"

"I can't remember them," the child murmured.

"Of course you can. Come on now. 'Our Father—' "

Stumblingly Lucy began the familiar words. Celia's eyes were on the clasped hands and tightly shut eyes and her brain followed only subconsciously the time-honoured words until, with a jerk, she realized something was wrong. Eva's head had snapped up and Lucy's eyes flew open. To her baffled anxiety Celia saw undeniable fear move in them. "*What* did you say?" she demanded.

Lucy's face flushed and then whitened. "I told you I'd forgotten it."

"But what was it you said?" The child did not answer but obediently, like a tape recorder, Celia's memory played back the words she had only subconsciously registered. "Lead us into temptation and deliver us to evil."

A wave of fear out of all proportion to the incident engulfed her and she wildly wished that Tom were home. With a supreme effort she held her voice steady. "Now start again and this time concentrate on what you're saying. I don't know what God will think of a prayer like that."

"He doesn't listen anyway," Lucy said under her breath.

"Of course he does. He hears every word you say."

"He can't when he's so far away, especially if other children are saying their prayers at the same time. He can't hear *everyone.*"

"I'm waiting, Lucy." Celia felt completely inadequate to embark on a theological discussion which in any case the child was obviously not disposed to listen to at the moment. As Lucy sulkily went through the prayer again, her mother resolved to reopen the subject when they were alone and need not be conscious, as she knew they both were, of Eva's unobtrusive but tense presence across the room.

During that month, of course, Lucy's piano lessons were continuing and now that it was dark so early Celia needed the car to take her to Front Street. She found herself alternately dreading the lessons and longing for them with a restless sense of impatience. They formed a chain in her mind, each one separate from and yet the same as the others, a link binding herself and Lucy ever more closely to Lucas Todd.

Toward the end of October, however, there was an incident which distinguished one lesson from the others. As usual Lucy was playing fluidly with Lucas unmoving beside her, while Celia flicked unseeingly through the glossy magazines which he invariably laid out for parents who accompanied their children to their lessons. Suddenly, above the music, the doorbell rang, its short, sharp note sounding an alarm. As though it was a signal, Lucy immediately stopped playing, and in the ensuing silence the sound reached them of footsteps on the stairs. As the front door was always on the latch, a perfunctory ring followed by entry was the recognized procedure for expected callers at the flat and Celia glanced at her watch, wondering for a moment if the lesson was running late and the next pupil had arrived. Reassured, she saw that there was another half hour to go, and with Lucy and Lucas she turned expectantly to the door. There

89

was a brief tap and a girl came hurrying into the room, stopping short on seeing the three of them silently awaiting her.

"Oh—I'm sorry," she stammered, a tide of colour flooding her face. "I didn't realize you had company."

"Can I help you?" Lucas enquired, and something in his voice—a warning or threat, she couldn't be sure—raised the hairs on Celia's scalp.

"No—no, it doesn't matter. I'm sorry. I'll call back later."

"I think not," Lucas said smoothly, still with the undercurrent vibrating through his words. "Please say what you came to say so that we may continue with our lesson."

Helplessly the girl's distressed eyes flicked to Celia and, aware of pity and anger, she rose to her feet. "It's all right, Lucy and I will wait outside for a minute."

"No—" Lucas began, but the girl's grateful "Thank you" cut across his words. Reluctantly Lucy slid off the piano stool and left the room with her mother. The girl had looked vaguely familiar but Celia couldn't place her. She realized suddenly that additional awkwardness had been caused by Lucas's remarkable failure to introduce them. In someone so punctiliously polite the oversight could only be deliberate.

"Do you know who that lady is, Lucy?" she asked on impulse.

"Yes, she's one of the teachers at school. Miss Delamere."

"What does she teach?"

"Art." Lucy moved impatiently. "She's wasting my lesson."

"I'm sure Mr. Todd will make up the time."

In fact there was very little to make up. As she finished speaking the door opened again and the girl came running out, tears streaming down her face. To Celia's relief she went hurrying down the stairs without seeming to notice them at the end of the hall. Anxiously she glanced down at Lucy, to whom adult tears must surely be a novelty, but the child's face was oddly dispassionate. Without speaking they went back together into the room. Lucas Todd was standing with his back to them looking out of the window and Celia was immediately aware of his intense anger.

After a moment he turned, said formally, "I apologize for the interruption," and nodded to Lucy to resume her playing. This she did instantly and after a moment or two the tension went out of him. He relaxed and turned to smile across at Celia. There was such unexpected warmth and intimacy in the smile that she found herself immediately responding, with an eagerness she found faintly embarrassing. It reminded her of schooldays, when one of the girls had been punished and the mistress seemed to go out of her way to be pleasant to the rest of the class. Though why he should wish to punish poor, frightened little Miss Delamere Celia could not imagine.

The following evening Eva went out, without as usual any explanation, and Celia looked forward to enjoying a comfortable evening alone with Tom. But immediately the meal was over he went to his desk, took a pile of books from his briefcase and sat down with his back to her. Since the radio or television would disturb him and they were clearly not going to have any conversation, she picked up her library book with a faintly aggrieved sense of disappointment. For an hour or more the only sounds in the room were the shifting logs in the grate, the rustle of turning pages and the scratching of Tom's pen. Suddenly, loud in the house, a terrified scream rang out.

They both leapt to their feet and, as Celia gasped "Kate!" they rushed to the door and up the stairs to the children's room. Kate was sitting up in bed, eyes staring and both hands crammed into her mouth.

"Darling, whatever's the matter?" Celia flung herself on the bed and pulled the shaking child against her. "What frightened you?"

"There was a witch looking at me through the window," Kate sobbed.

"Nonsense, darling, you were dreaming."

"No, I saw her! She had long grey hair and a hooked nose and there was a cat on her shoulder."

"Hush, sweetheart, there's nothing there."

"There was, I tell you. It's Hallowe'en and that's when all the witches fly about. Eva said so."

"Then she should have had more sense," Celia said tightly.

Kate caught hold of her dress and strained closer to her mother. "And she said there were spirits and ghosts about tonight, too, and magic everywhere. Mummy, I don't want to see a ghost! Please don't let me!"

"Of course you won't see a ghost." Soothingly Celia stroked the dark head. The plaits had worked loose and soft hair rippled over the child's shoulders.

"I'm not afraid," Lucy said unexpectedly from the other bed. "Kate's a crybaby. I wouldn't mind seeing a witch."

"I bet you would!" Kate cried, the tears starting again.

"Anyway," Lucy finished, humping under the bedclothes, "Eva was talking to me. You shouldn't have listened if it frightened you."

Tom, having satisfied himself that his daughter was un-hurt, returned to the study and was bent over his papers when, ten minutes later, Celia rejoined him.

"Of all the irresponsible things to do!" she burst out. "Fancy filling the child's head with all that superstitious twaddle! You'd think she'd know better." Tom merely

92

grunted in reply. "I'm rapidly getting to the stage when I've had quite enough of my dear stepsister."

"Because she tells the children fairy stories?"

"Because she scares them half to death."

"Not Lucy, apparently."

"No," Celia agreed consideringly, "not Lucy. That's another thing. The child's changed since Eva came. She's— harder, more stubborn and defiant."

"Which no doubt is also Eva's fault."

"Yes, I think it is."

"Oh Celia, be logical! Eva's to blame because Kate's frightened and she's also to blame because Lucy isn't! She can't win, poor girl!"

"There's something sly and underhand about her which I just don't trust somehow."

"You're not harking back to that infernal tie pin, are you?"

"Tom, you remember insisting that this arrangement was only to be temporary, and we could send her back to Angie if things got too much for me?"

"All I remember is Angie blaming the girl for Ruth failing 0-levels and Martin dropping out, which is about as ludicrous as the way you're carrying on now."

"But you did say it depended on me."

"What if I did?"

She drew a deep breath. "Well, I want to send her back."

He turned slowly from the desk to face her. "You're not serious, surely?"

"Yes, I am. Quite serious."

"You mean to say that because Kate has a nightmare one night, Eva has to go?"

"That's only the final straw."

"What else has she done? Well?" as she hesitated. "Come

on. In all conscience there must be *something* else."

"She hasn't fitted in as well as I'd hoped."

"On the contrary, she's perfectly at home."

"You said yourself you'd never liked her and you were right."

"Oh nonsense, I was mistaken. I never really knew her, that's all. She's a quiet, pleasant little thing and you said yourself how good she is with Lucy. The child worships her."

"Don't use that word!" Celia said sharply.

He slammed down his pen. "*Now* what's the matter?"

"I told you about Lucy's prayers. I'm sure, from the way she reacted, that Eva was behind that too."

"Good heavens, you really mean it, don't you? You've chalked up all the stupid, meaningless things you can think of and the total adds up to the fact that Eva must go! If it wasn't so pathetic it would be funny."

"If you think it's funny when your daughter prays to be delivered to evil—"

"*Celia!* Now that's quite enough! You can't honestly believe that a kid's harmless mixup of words has anything sinister about it? Surely even you aren't as neurotic as that!"

"*Even* I, Tom?"

They were facing each other now, flushed and angry. Miserably Celia thought: It wasn't like this before Eva came.

"You know what I mean. You seem to go out of your way looking for things. The girl can't do anything right. You didn't like her going to Lucas's flat when she was only trying to be of help. You were ready on the flimsiest evidence to accuse her of stealing the ashtray and later my old tie pin. You say there's something 'unhealthy' about her obvious admiration for Lucas and now you're flying off the handle because she's been telling the children fairy tales. Can't you

94

see how twisted you're becoming? Any day now you'll be as bad as Angie!"

"There's no need to speak of Angie like that," Celia said coldly.

"Well, honestly! If it's not Eva you're tilting at, it's Lucas himself. For some strange reason you don't like him, either. Really, Celia, I don't know what's got into you lately!"

She had opened her mouth to reply when they became joltingly aware that the door had opened and Eva was standing quietly looking at them. Just for a second, before their habitual blind came down, Celia was sure she detected triumph in the girl's eyes.

"I'm sorry," she murmured self-effacingly, "I just wanted to tell you I'm in. I think I'll go straight up to bed."

"Oh nonsense. Come in, Eva," Tom said heartily. "Wouldn't you like a hot drink or something? It's pretty nippy out there." He reached for her hand. "As I thought—you're frozen."

"I'm all right, really," she answered softly, smiling up at him and letting her hand lie in his. "You've enough to think about without worrying about me."

"But of course I worry about you! You're part of the family, after all."

Celia said stridently, "If she doesn't want a drink there's no point in forcing her. If she does, she's capable of making it herself."

Eva hastily removed her hand from Tom's with, Celia felt, an unnecessary display of confusion. "Yes, Celia's quite right. I only looked in to say good-night." And with a sweet, vague smile she slipped from the room.

"There's no knowing how much she heard," Tom said flatly.

"Well, whatever it was, the matter won't be helped by standing like an idiot holding her hand!"

Tom flushed darkly. "Of all the—"

"I'm going to bed too," she said in a rush, and almost ran from the room. On the landing she paused and glanced broodingly at the half-closed door up the short flight of steps. For a moment she thought she could detect the smell of candles again. Then, as she still stood on the landing, the door softly closed. Miserably Celia turned into her own room.

CHAPTER 8

THE phone call came at six o'clock on a Saturday morning. Celia awoke with the panic that its jangle always arouses during the hours of sleep. "Yes, what is it?" She was fumbling up the wall as she spoke, scrabbling for the light switch, sure it was still the middle of the night.

"Sergeant Dunstable here, Mrs. Bannerman. Sorry to disturb you. Could I have a word with your husband?"

She blinked in the sudden deluge of light. "Yes—yes, of course. Tom." She turned, thrusting the instrument into his sleep-warm hand. He struggled up on one elbow. "Hello, yes? Bannerman here."

Six o'clock, Celia thought. Whatever can it be? Has the school been broken into, burned down?

"*What?*" The horror in Tom's voice scored a shudder down her spine. "Oh, no! How did they find her? . . . I've no idea. Yes, I'll come at once. Give me ten minutes to throw some clothes on." He reached over her to drop the phone back on its rest and his eyes came down to her startled enquiring face.

"Frances Delamere," he said briefly. "Her body's been washed up on the beach."

"Frances—?" Memory struck with the picture of the girl running in tears from the flat on Front Street. "Oh no!"

Tom was already pulling off his pyjama jacket. "They don't know if she has any relatives in the area. I doubt it, I think she's in digs in the town. She's only been with us a couple of terms. A nice kid. I can't imagine how it happened. Perhaps they'll know more by the time I get there. As if I hadn't enough on my plate without this."

"Will you be back for breakfast?"

"I've no idea. I'll stay as long as I can be of any help. Lord, what a mess!" He tucked a cravat into the neck of his shirt and pulled on a sweater. "The thought of her in that cold, dark water—"

"Don't!" Celia said violently.

"Sorry, it's not pleasant. You didn't know her, though, did you?"

"I saw her once." She didn't elaborate.

"Well, I'll see you later."

The door swung to behind him. Celia shivered and drew the bedclothes up over her shoulders. Cold, dark water—She thought of Lucas's pointed lack of civility, his anger after the girl had gone. Why had she visited him in such agitation? Had her distress that evening ten days ago any connection with today's tragedy?

It was a damp, misty November day. Tom reappeared, pale and on edge, for breakfast and then shut himself in the study telephoning anyone who might know where Frances Delamere's relatives could be found. It transpired that she had no close family, merely an aged aunt living in Cumberland. Since she could hardly be expected to travel down to identify the body, it seemed that Tom must do it. This he accepted with a passive resignation.

The hours crawled by. Celia had accepted Eva's offer to do the weekend shopping and busied herself with some mending which had been accumulating. Morning slid into

98

afternoon. Beyond the warm pool of the study, greyness lay heavily outside the windows. Dank and dripping, the naked trees stood dejectedly with drooping branches. Kate was curled up in one of the deep armchairs, buried in *Treasure Island*. Lucy lay on her stomach on the floor with a jigsaw puzzle spread out before her. Every now and then Eva, dropping her knitting in her lap, leant forward to suggest a piece to try. Presumably Tom was either at the mortuary or the police station. The warmth and the electric light which had been necessary all day combined to give Celia a headache. She stood up suddenly.

"I'm going for a walk."

Kate looked up blankly. "In this weather?"

"I just want to get out of the house for a while. Will you see to tea, Eva, if I'm not back?"

"Of course." Eva's dark eyes, huge under the thick fringe of hair, were consideringly on her face. Celia found she could not meet them.

"I don't suppose I'll be long." She left the room, shivering at the drop of temperature in the hall. She took down her heavy winter coat from the peg, checked that gloves were in the pocket, and let herself out of the dark house. At the gate she glanced back. The light from the study window was a diffused blur in the mist. She pulled the gate shut, turned up the collar of her coat and crossed the road quickly. In the park the paths were treacherous with slippery wet leaves. A squirrel stopped and peered at her, its tail bedraggled and limp, the fur plastered to its body. Head down, Celia walked quickly, trying to escape from the miserable fancies which had been afflicting her all day.

People were about in the High Street. The wet streets shimmered with reflected light and the shop windows were full of tempting displays of Christmas merchandise. She turned into Smugglers' Walk, glancing in the windows of the small boutiques and antique shops which lined it, drearily wondering what she could buy Angie and Melanie—and Eva —for Christmas.

In Water Lane the school presented her with a grey, dripping face, as though in mourning for the member who would never again walk through its gates. Celia shivered and on impulse turned her back on the school and the continuation of Smugglers' Walk and hurried further along Water Lane until she came to the corner of Cobble Way. This was where Eva had brought the children to see the fortune teller all those weeks ago. More slowly now Celia went down the narrow, uneven pavements. Small old houses crowded together, their front doors opening directly on the foot path, their round dark windows lining her progress with suspicious sightless eyes. It was hard to distinguish one house from another and in any case she didn't know the number of the fortune teller's. She wondered whether Eva had been again since, and imagined the scene behind one of those small, grimy windows—the rickety card table sheeted in black or purple silk and the brightly coloured cards scattered on it like a collection of shining jewels.

The little lane ended in Front Street, not the dignified end that she knew, with the gracious, rather old-fashioned hotels and flats, but an altogether tawdrier part, admittedly not at its best on this dank November day. The railings along the sea side of the road were only just visible through the misty rain which even now, at just after three o'clock, was becoming tinged with the blue of premature darkness. Gaps in them indicated the steep steps leading down to the promenade. Had Frances Delamere gone down them, knowing very well she would never come up again?

Hastily Celia averted her eyes from the grey space on the

100

other side of the road. To her left souvenir shops and cheap cafés were boarded up for their hibernation until next season and someone had scrawled obscenities in red paint over the closed wooden faces.

Smugglers' Walk opened beside her and she hesitated. The sensible thing would be to go back up it to the more cheerful, peopled High Street and perhaps drop into Rawdons for a pot of tea and a toasted teacake. It seemed almost unbelievable, here on this deserted street, that people were actually hurrying about up there, happily shopping and having tea.

Almost against her will, Celia found she had crossed the bottom of Smugglers' Walk and was continuing along Front Street. Somewhere on the shrouded sea a foghorn lowed mournfully. She crossed over and stood staring out beyond the railings, straining to penetrate the drifting barriers of mist. And beside her Lucas Todd said quietly, "You look in need of a hot drink."

There was no surprise in her. Tacitly she now knew she had come down here expressly to meet him. She said unevenly, "Did you see Frances Delamere last night?"

"I did."

She turned to look at him. Although he was only slightly taller than she, the light-coloured mack he wore accentuated his height as it did his sallowness. It was the first time she had seen him in anything but dark colours.

"She came to the flat?"

"Yes."

"Why?"

He smiled slightly, his tawny eyes searching hers. "Why have you come?"

His question took her by surprise. "I needed some air. It was hot in the house."

"Perhaps," he said quietly, "it was also hot in her house."

"But she drowned herself!" Celia cried harshly.

"Yes. There was nothing I could do for her."

She forced herself to meet his eyes. "What can you do for me, Lucas?"

"A great deal, if you will let me. More than you—dream of." His hesitation before the word "dream" again suggested that he knew she continually dreamed about him—even, perhaps, what she dreamed. His lips would be cold, she thought confusedly, colder than the fog, and she longed to touch them. A kind of mindless acceptance began to lap over her. Tom was out. The children were safe enough for the moment with Eva. For once she had time to spare and an undeniable need to know this man better, this man who, in two short months, had come to dominate their lives. A ripple of anticipation chased over her skin. He said softly, "You are cold. Perhaps you are ready now for another warm house."

It would have been natural in the circumstances to have taken her arm as she had seen him take Mrs. Bannerman's and to lead her back toward the flat. But he made no attempt to touch her and side by side they moved up the road, crossed it and entered the familiar doorway. The thought passed through her mind that she was not being very discreet, that she had never before been alone with him, but excitement was moving inside her and she just did not care.

The flat was strange without Lucy. Almost at once he laid a silver tray on the table by the fire where usually the glossy magazines were displayed, and the teacake she had desired fifteen minutes before now awaited her, dripping with butter. She raised her eyes to his face.

"You were expecting me."

"Of course."

"How did you know I would come?"

"It was inevitable."

102

She said suddenly, "Tom and I seem to be finding a lot to argue about lately."

"That too is inevitable."

"Why?" she asked curiously.

He shrugged. "Tom is too solid, too down to earth for anyone like you. He has already gone as far up the ladder as he is capable. The Tarot cards indicated as much. He was headmaster at thirty-eight, was he not? It was admirable but he has nowhere else to go."

His words seeped into her mind soothingly like a tide of warm honey, their tone rather than their content lulling away her doubts and worries. At the same time she half-wondered whether he was actually speaking at all, or whether their communication was completely mental.

"And I?"

"Could be a great violinist. You know that."

She shook her head sadly. "Not any more. I haven't played for years."

"But you could. Think of the progress young Lucy has made in a few short weeks."

"You would teach me?"

"Naturally."

"But I thought the piano was your instrument?"

"Forgive me, my dear, but I could also teach you more about the violin than you have ever known."

"And what would be the price of the lessons?"

Tawny eyes, compelling eyes, all-knowing eyes. "We could discuss that later."

On the mantelpiece the tiny ivory clock whirred and struck.

"I ought to be going."

"I believe you want to stay."

"About Tom: you mentioned the Tarot."

"It told the truth. If you remain tied to him he will hold you back."

The voice of the serpent, the tempter. To shut it out she said quickly, "Play for me."

"Of course." He moved over to the piano and opened the rosewood lid, trailing his fingers over the keys, and it seemed to her that it was her soul he was fingering so delicately, causing it to vibrate to the tune that he willed.

She leant back in the chair and closed her eyes and the music crept across the room to claim her. For a while, passively, she gave herself up to it. Then, with rising excitement, she felt him moving toward her, felt his long fingers caressing her hair, her throat, her breast, the coldness of his lips brushing against hers. With a strangled little cry she reached up to pull him closer, but her hands touched only empty air. Confused and trembling she opened her eyes. He was still at the piano, as of course he must have remained since there had been no break in the music. And she remembered hotly how her deepest longings had always filled her mind when he played. His coming to her had only been one of them, a tantalizing wish-fulfillment, nothing more.

But now his figure at the piano seemed far away and the space between them stretched ever more taut like a piece of elastic that would surely snap, jerking them together. She thought of the vast room of her dream and how against her will she had been drawn across it toward him. Almost without knowing it she was on her feet and moving slowly, fluidly across the endlessly stretching floor. The sharp corner of the piano dug into her outstretched palm before she realized she had reached it. Frantically she wrenched her mind clear of the wafting, sticky threads which, spiderlike, were threatening to enclose it.

"Why do you play this game with me?" she cried wildly.

104

"How can I know whether or not you want me?"

He stopped playing abruptly and she gave a little moan, needing the balm of the music, suffering instant pangs of withdrawal. He said softly, "Wanting someone is not wholly physical, Celia. Possession of the body is a temporary thing."

"And does not interest you?"

"No. Forgive me."

"Then what do you want from me?"

He turned and looked up at her, his eyes pools of golden light in the dimness of the room. "How does it go in the Good Book?" he asked mockingly. " 'Heart and soul and mind and strength'?"

She said jerkily, " 'The devil can cite scripture for his purpose.' "

She was conscious that for the first time she had surprised him. He smiled slowly, light flooding over his face. "Power, Celia, that is what I offer you. Mastery of the violin but even more, over the people who hear you play. You have it in you, as Lucy has. It only needs to be developed and released." His eyes dropped to her finger, which as always when disturbed she was rubbing.

"And the price?" she whispered fearfully.

He said oddly, "You have already started to pay."

"Not, please God, like Frances Delamere did."

A frown crossed his face and was gone. "She was an impressionable child."

"Who fell in love with you? Why do you despise love so much, Lucas, when you set out to make yourself indispensable to people?"

"I do not despise love of the right kind."

"But hers was the wrong kind and became a nuisance." He did not reply. Quite suddenly her mind was shatteringly clear. "She didn't realize, did she, the price she would be called on to pay? What did you use as bait? The promise that she would become a great artist? But she ruined everything by falling in love with you. That was clearly an impossible situation—wasn't it?"

His eyes were fixed on hers, intent, probing.

"You tried to tell her it was impossible but she wouldn't believe you. Poor girl, she took your interest in her at face value. So, since she refused to accept your prevarications, you had no option but to tell her the truth."

She could feel his excitement stirring, rising, bursting out of him, but he did not move. Only a tiny pulse at the corner of his temple beat a steady, impassioned tattoo. "And of course her mind snapped. When she realized what she had come to love she ran straight out of the flat and into the sea."

His tongue flicked out over his lips. She pursued relentlessly, "That's what happened, isn't it?"

"Bravo!" The voice might have been in her own head.

She said in a whisper, "How evil you are! Cold and ruthless and totally without mercy."

"But it strikes a responsive chord in you, does it not?" He reached out at last and took her hand and she steeled herself against the wave of shuddering, revolted desire which engulfed her. "Celia, you could be as ruthless as I if you schooled yourself to it. There is no limit to the power I can give you." His finger rubbed convulsively against the hard core of skin on hers and suddenly he raised her hand swiftly and his mouth closed on it. Feverishly she tried to pull it away, feeling, terrified, the force of his tongue as he sucked at her finger. She thought: He's insane, and so am I!

He looked up, his face gleaming with sweat, his eyes molten amber. "Do you not know yet that it was for you I came? For you and Lucy?"

"No!" The word shuddered out of her. She twisted her

106

hand from his grip, stumbled dizzily to the door, catching up her coat from the back of the chair where she had dropped it. He made no move to stop her. Her legs were as heavy as tree trunks, as clumsy as a robot's. Somehow, clinging to the banisters, she went clattering down the stairs and out into the breath-stopping coldness of the night.

Like a creature demented she ran crazily, swerving backwards and forwards across the road, sobbing and coughing with terror when her zigzag flight brought her up sharp before a flight of steps leading down to the sea—and oblivion. She spun round, hurling herself forward, spendthrift in the energy she wasted, intent only on escape. Up Smugglers' Walk, the shops closed now for the night. A man leaning against a corner said something but she didn't hear. Gasping, choking against shortage of breath and the searing pain in her side, she wove her erratic progress up to the High Street. The park gates had been locked with the fall of darkness and it was necessary to go the longer way home up Regent's Walk and along Cavendish Road.

As she staggered against her own gate a shadow detached itself from the light at the study window, the front door burst open and Tom rushed down the path towards her. "Celia! For pity's sake where have you been? What in the name of heaven happened to you?"

Dazedly she looked down at her unfastened coat, the mist lying heavy and wet on her woolen dress. She let him lead her inside, straight into the study and down on to one of the low, comfortable, comforting chairs. As he moved quickly to the drinks cabinet, Eva knelt before her and began to remove her boots. "You know, don't you?" she said softly, her eyes like live coals in the pallor of her face.

Tom thrust a glass into Celia's hand and she drank it quickly, almost retching as the fiery liquid seared down her throat and into her deeply chilled body. He removed the empty glass and laid it down. Then he took her cold hands in his and chafed them warm. Her finger was red and a little swollen from the force of Lucas's mouth. A tremor ran through her and she turned her face against the wing of the chair.

"Where did you go?" Tom demanded. "It got later and later. I phoned Angie and Melanie but they hadn't seen you." He gave a brief, mirthless laugh. "I was beginning to wonder if I wouldn't be called upon to identify another pathetic, dripping body taken from the sea."

She turned back then, her eyes moving slowly over his face, pitying the tension and worry she read in it. "It was a near thing," she said.

CHAPTER 9

THE clarity which had enabled Celia to accuse
Lucas had clouded by the next morning and even the time
she had spent in his flat was hazy. Had she ever actually gone
there, or was it another of those lifelike dreams which continually plagued her? Her mind went back instead to the
feeling of doom with which she had awoken on the sunny
September day when both Lucas and Eva came into her life.
The forces of evil closing in, she thought fatalistically.

"Tom, will you come to church with me this morning?"

He turned in surprise. "What brought that on? Surely
Mother's coming to lunch as usual?"

"If I get up now I can leave things ready before we go."

"It would be a bit of a rush, wouldn't it?"

She sighed, letting the resolution fade. "Yes, I suppose it
would. Never mind."

He reached out for her hand and she winced as his fingers
brushed against her tender one. "There'll be a memorial
service for Frances," he said gently, thinking he had detected
the reason for her desire. "We'll go to that as soon as it can
be arranged."

But it wasn't a memorial service she needed, it was an
amulet, a charm to ward off the evil spirits. Deliver us *from*,
not to, evil. She tried to pray silently but the words eluded

109

her as they had Lucy. *It was for you I came, you and Lucy.*

She heard herself say, "She was at Lucas's flat on Friday night."

Tom released her hand. "Frances was?"

"Yes. He must have been the last person to see her alive."

"Person?" Was he a person? Lucy insisted he had no aura. She pushed aside the nebulous questioning. "Perhaps the police ought to see him."

"Oh, I don't think that's necessary. It was suicide, they're sure of that. There wasn't a mark on her, and although there's to be a post-mortem they're pretty sure they can rule out drugs or poison of any kind. She quite simply drowned herself."

"Why?" she asked flatly.

"Heaven knows. A love affair, perhaps, that went wrong."

"She loved Lucas."

He looked at her curiously. "What makes you say that?"

"I just know she did."

"Well, you could be right. It doesn't make him guilty of her death, though, poor chap."

"Doesn't it?"

"Oh Celia, grow up! If he couldn't reciprocate, he couldn't. He'd have no reason to think she'd go and kill herself."

"I'm not so sure."

"*I'm* sure. You really have got it in for him, haven't you, him and Eva? It's not like you to take such violent dislikes to people."

"He's evil, Tom. Don't you feel it?"

"*Evil?* For heaven's sake!"

"I don't want Lucy to have anything more to do with him. If you remember, I was against it in the first place. I'm only sorry I let you talk me round."

110

"We're not back on that old tack, surely? Have you forgotten that two months ago Lucy didn't know one note from another? And look at her now."

"I know. It's—abnormal. Paranormal, anyway."

He shook his head despairingly. "I don't understand you at all. Are you actually complaining because your faith in her ability has been proved right?"

"Please, Tom. I know you don't understand but please believe me that it's vitally important, to all of us. I wouldn't ask you if it weren't, but I want you to promise me that you'll dismiss Lucas at the end of this term."

"Dismiss him? Dismiss the best music master I've ever had, and after all the trouble I had finding anyone at all? Are you out of your mind?"

"Perhaps I am. I know you were desperate to find someone, perhaps too desperate."

"You speak in riddles these days. What's that supposed to mean?"

"You offered to sell your soul for a music master. Suppose someone took you up on that?"

After a moment he wiped his hand across his face. "Am I going mad, or are you?"

"I remember you coming home that night and pulling me into a dance of triumph. 'Our prayers have been answered!' you said. But if they were prayers, they were unholy ones."

"Celia—look, love, I don't know what's got into you, but I don't like it. All this talk of evil and unholy prayers—Try to be rational. You don't like Lucas. Okay. You don't have to. But that's no reason to make him out to be the devil incarnate." She caught her breath sharply. "Apart from anything else," Tom was going on, "I like the chap. He's good for my morale."

"But not your morals."

"Oh, I don't know. At least I haven't started raiding the school fund yet. But seriously, when I'm with him I feel calm and confident and capable of knocking down houses if they stood in my way. I think he has faith in me."

Oh Tom, she thought despairingly, he despises you! Despises you and writes you off without so much as a backward glance.

"Come to that," he added a little defiantly, "Eva has the same effect. Bolsters up my ego, somehow, when it starts to wilt."

"Despite the future she mapped out for you?"

"Oh that—it was just a game. But try not to be quite so sharp with her, will you love? She's a sensitive little thing and I can tell it hurts her."

Sweet, simpering, helpless little Eva, playing up to big, strong, protective Tom! Would men never realize how easy it was to gain control of them? "We'd better get up," she said heavily.

For the next day or two, Eva seemed to be watching Celia with an air of expectancy that she found both puzzling and unnerving. She tried to close her mind to it but it remained just below the surface, needling and irritating and undermining the concentration which she felt increasingly she should be centering on Lucy. One particular instance at that time caused her deep disquiet. She was upstairs tidying some drawers one evening after tea when she suddenly felt a vital, imperative need to find Lucy. For a few moments she attempted to withstand it. Lucy was safely downstairs—she had seen her only ten minutes ago. But the compulsion was not to be denied. She ran quickly down the stairs and pushed open the study door. For a moment there was complete silence, then Kate started to laugh and clap her hands. Celia looked sharply from her to Lucy's flushed, triumphant face.

112

Eva, as usual, had her head discreetly bent over a book.

"What's the matter?" she demanded. "What are you laughing at?"

"Lucy said she could make you come downstairs, and she did!"

An iron vise seemed to close round Celia and begin to tighten. "What are you talking about?"

"I said she couldn't do it, but she did!"

"That's ridiculous," Celia disclaimed faintly. "I was coming down anyway."

"Then what did you come in here for?" Lucy's eyes, suddenly much older than a six-year-old's, held hers across the room. Lucy has the power, as I have, and she has already started to develop hers. She "wished" people to be ill, she "wished" to improve her piano playing. Celia's own power, if indeed she had any, lay dormant and untapped. If she were to be strong enough to withstand Lucy, to withstand her so as to be able to help her, perhaps she should begin to exercise power of her own. But where did the power come from? Lucas Todd? She wanted nothing that was his.

"Stop picking your finger, Lucy!" she said sharply, and felt Eva's eyes musingly on her face. That odd little lump on the child's finger, identical to her own; the first time he came to the house, Lucas had stroked it. Had he ever, perhaps in the privacy of the music cubicles at school, had her hand in his mouth? A ripple of horror zigzagged through her body and, dignified in her defeat, she turned and left the room.

Panic had welled in her at the prospect of Lucy's next music lesson, but she no longer contemplated keeping her from it. Lucas and Lucy were too strong for that. In the event, as had happened before, Lucas was as circumspect as ever, yet there was in his manner a subtle hint of intimacy, almost as though on her last visit they had become lovers.

113

Self-consciously she kept her right hand out of sight as much as possible—in a glove, under a magazine, behind her back, and the stratagem was not helped by the fact that the moment she entered the flat her finger had started to itch and burn as though it needed the coldness of his mouth to quench the discomfort. But if Lucas noticed her uneasiness he gave no sign of it and the lesson passed without incident.

A few days later Martin drifted round again. Celia was mixing Christmas puddings and the kitchen table was covered in flour, spices and packets of dried fruit.

"How are things?" she asked him, remembering his misery on his last visit.

"Much the same. There's the hell of an atmosphere at home. I thought it might die down once Eva had gone but if anything it's worse. Even Ruth seems odd these days. She was sick the other night but when I asked her about it in the morning, she denied it." He glanced at her surreptitiously. "How are things with you?"

"Oh—all right, I suppose."

"And Uncle Tom?"

"All right too."

His mouth twisted. "No sign of the death and disaster Eva so kindly prophesied for him?"

"Not as yet. At least—there has been a death."

"Oh yes, Miss Delamere. Ruth was talking about it. Celia —" It was always "Uncle Tom" but it was years since he had called her "aunt."

"Yes?"

"You are—happy, aren't you? With Uncle, I mean."

She looked across at him. "That's a funny question."

He flushed. "I'm sorry. It's just—I don't know, I was afraid that perhaps you weren't. It's probably harking back

114

to those infernal cards again, and everyone seems to be bickering at each other these days."

She said slowly, "Is there any particular reason why you should think we might not be happy?"

He turned away quickly. "No, no. Nothing definite."

"So there's nothing specific you want to tell me?"

After a moment he shook his head. Celia let out her held breath in a long sigh and reached for the cinnamon. "Any more thoughts about University?"

"No. I've had it for this year, at least."

"Uncle would be glad to discuss it with you if you have second thoughts and feel you can't talk to your parents."

"Thanks," he said gruffly. "Well, I'd better go. Mum's certainly making what use she can of me. I've a shopping list a yard long!" He smiled fleetingly. "By the way—" It was painfully casual, yet in all probability it was the real reason for his visit—"how's Eva these days? I've almost forgotten what she looks like!"

Celia said bitterly, "No one but Eva herself ever knows how she is."

"No. Well, I must go." Suddenly to her amazement he came round the table, slipped an awkward arm round her waist and kissed her cheek. It was a boy's kiss, clumsy, misfiring slightly, but it was the first unsolicited one he had ever given her.

"Goodbye," he mumbled, and fled, leaving her standing at the table with the wooden spoon in her hand and her eyes full of tears.

"Don't forget the school barn dance next week," Tom remarked at dinner one evening.

"Oh dear, has that come round again?"

115

"Can we go, Daddy?" Kate pleaded.

"Sorry, honey, you're not old enough. Fourteen's the minimum age."

"But why? It's not fair!"

"Because it goes on quite late, that's why. At your age you need your sleep."

"But it's on a Friday. We could stay in bed late the next morning!"

"Sorry, Kate, I don't make the rules, the P.A. does."

"But you're President of the P.A.," Kate returned sulkily.

Celia said quietly, "You're going ahead with it, then?"

"We thought it was best to carry on." Poor Frances Delamere would never dance again.

As the day drew nearer, Celia acknowledged to herself that she didn't want to go to the dance. She had been increasingly tired and listless all week and she longed for a quiet evening in which to relax and go to bed early. The thought of all the wild hilarity, the clapping hands and stamping feet, was anathema to her.

"Tom," she began diffidently when he arrived home that evening, "I really don't feel up to the dance tonight. Would you mind very much if I don't go?"

He moved past her into the study, his face drawn, and poured himself a stiff drink.

"I know I really ought to go, but I haven't been sleeping very well—"

"Um?" He turned to face her, draining the glass in one gulp, and she realized with a faint shock that he hadn't heard what she had been saying.

"Tom, what is it? What's happened?"

He went quickly to the door, glanced into the hall, then shut the door and leant against it, running his fingers worriedly through his hair. "I'll tell you what's happened. The

116

thing I've always dreaded. Some of the kids have been experimenting with dope."

She stared at him whitely. "How do you know?"

"Jack Barlow's suspected it for some time. Today he went down to the cloakrooms during break, when they should all have been outside. He caught them at it."

"Reefers?"

"Mainly, I think. What frightened the life out of him, though, was that he found a syringe under one of the benches. No one would admit to having seen it before."

"You mean it could be hard drugs?"

"I don't know. I'm not well up on this. It's something I've always played ostrich about—the one thing I've always felt would be beyond my control."

"What are you going to do?"

"If it's hard drugs I've no option but to hand it over to the police. I had a long talk on the phone with Alan and he's coming round here tomorrow morning. If I didn't have to go to this bloody dance tonight, he could have come straight away."

"And what about the boys concerned? Have you been in touch with their parents?"

Tom glanced at her and moved back to the drinks cabinet. "There were more girls than boys involved." He poured himself a stiff whisky and drank it straight. "I suppose you'll have to know so I might as well tell you now. The word is that Ruth was behind it."

"*Ruth?*" Celia's voice cracked. "She was one of them?"

"Not only that. According to a girl who panicked, Ruth was the instigator."

Celia said in a whisper, "It will just about kill Angie." Only later did it strike her that she had accepted Ruth's involvement without question. Martin said she had been sick

117

in the night—and Ruth had been exposed to Eva for almost a year. She didn't doubt Angie would lay the blame on Eva, and this time she was only too ready to concede she could be right.

Tom glanced at his watch. "I suppose I'd better get changed. I couldn't feel less like cavorting round like an idiot."

"I had been going to ask if you'd mind if I didn't go, but in the circumstances you'll need some support."

"It doesn't matter, if you don't feel up to it. Believe me, I'm only going because I have to. Anyway, Eva'll be there if I need to have my hand held."

Eva, who bolstered his ego. "Have you spoken to Michael?"

"No, I've not been in touch with any of the parents yet. For one thing it would have washed out the dance completely—most of them will be there—and we desperately need all the money we can get for school funds. And secondly I must have time to find the best way of approaching them. Some of them are quite likely to refuse to believe their child is involved."

"Poor Angie. This on top of Martin's defection."

"Yes, they're certainly having a rough year." His hand reached out again to the whisky bottle.

Celia said quickly, "Darling, don't you think you've had enough for now?"

"No, I bloody well don't." He sloshed the liquid into the glass.

"But you'll have to be pleasant to everyone—"

"All the more reason to build up my spirits."

"I'll come with you," she said quietly.

"No need. I shan't be dancing much, anyway. You're better out of it."

118

"Then I'll make you an omelet, as blotting paper. I suppose they'll serve hot dogs and things there."

"Don't bother, I couldn't swallow anything solid. At the moment I doubt if I'll ever be able to face food again."

"Tom—" She laid a hand on his arm, "try not to worry too much. Try to shelve it till you've a chance to thrash it out with Alan. He'll know what to do."

"Good advice, if I were only capable of taking it." He patted her hand and went upstairs to change. Celia moved nearer to the fire. Ruth, of all people being mixed up with drugs! She'd always understood it was only children from disturbed homes. But according to Martin, their home was disturbed, had been ever since Eva's arrival had first begun to spread the ripples of disharmony. Had Eva ever tried drugs herself? Impossible to know. Celia's heart ached for Tom, blundering into something he didn't understand. She was slightly apprehensive about the amount of alcohol he had consumed in so short a space of time. It was as well there would only be soft drinks at the dance—and she'd try to persuade him to let Eva drive.

This, as she might have expected, Tom would not agree to. "I'm perfectly sober," he said belligerently.

"Maybe, but you'd never pass a breathalizer and that's what counts."

"I'm not likely to meet one between here and Water Lane."

Eva said softly, "Don't worry, Celia, I'll look after him."

There was nothing more she could do. The front door closed behind them and she went to the kitchen to prepare the children's supper. Ruth—She couldn't believe that a child she'd known all its life—it could as easily be Kate.

Lucy was sitting at the table with a box of plasticine in

front of her, squeezing the pliable stuff between her stubby little fingers. Celia made an effort to be normal. "What are you making? A zoo?"

Lucy's eyes flashed to her mother's face and down again. "No, a school." She continued with her prodding and shaping, the tip of her tongue between her lips emphasizing her concentration.

"I thought you'd used the last of the plasticine you had for your birthday."

"Eva bought me some more."

Celia glanced a little dubiously at the squat figures lining up on the table. "Is it any particular school, one out of a book?"

"It's our school," Lucy said firmly. "This is Daddy, and that's Mr. Todd, and this one's Mr. Barlow and the one I'm doing now is Miss Lancer."

"Poor woman," Celia forced a laugh. There was nothing to account for her distaste for the row of figures and yet somehow she felt vaguely uneasy. "Look, there's one over here which has fallen into the egg-cup." She moved forward but Lucy's voice halted her.

"No!" she said quickly, "Don't move it. It's supposed to be there. It's Miss Delamere."

"Lucy!" Celia's horror-struck eyes stared down at the roughly modelled little figure which, she now saw, was lying head down in a few inches of water at the bottom of the egg-cup.

"She's drowned," Lucy explained unnecessarily.

"I think it's horrible. Please take it out at once. How can you be so—so callous?"

Sulkily, after a glance at her mother's white face, the child tipped the figure back onto the table.

"I don't think it's nice to make them real people, anyway,"

120

Celia said with an effort. "You've always made animals or characters out of books before."

"Eva says it's more fun to make real people," Lucy remarked casually. "She's got lots of little dolls upstairs in a box."

There was a darkness swimming in front of Celia's eyes. She reached blindly for a chair and lowered herself into it. "What—what kind of dolls?" She already knew the answer.

"Oh, all kinds. Some bought and some she made herself, out of plasticine or wax." The smell of candles. Celia felt nausea scorching the base of her throat. "They're very good and they have real hair and the right clothes, too."

"Real hair?"

"Yes, Eva gets it out of hairbrushes. So the doll like Daddy really has some of Daddy's hair. Isn't that clever?"

It couldn't—possibly—be true. Wild stories of voodoo and black magic flooded Celia's shrinking mind. But here, in twentieth-century Rychester—*in her own home!* Witchcraft is far more prevalent than most people suppose, Alan had said. And Eva had sat quietly listening, taut and secretive in her excitement.

She forced herself to say lightly, "Has Eva got dolls of the whole family, then?"

"Most of them, and some of the people at school, too."

"Well, you're not to do it, Lucy. I won't have you making real people like that. It's—obscene."

"Your doll has a bandage on its finger," Lucy remarked offhandedly. "I know you haven't really got one, but Eva said—"

Celia's hand slammed down on the table. "I don't want to hear what Eva said, or anything more about it. I'll speak to her myself, but you're not to go to her room ever again, do you hear?"

121

Lucy didn't reply but her mouth had set in a mutinous line. Hopelessly Celia knew it was impossible to enforce this rule. How could she ensure that the child never went into a room in her own house? Surely, when Tom heard all this he wouldn't stick up for Eva any more and would agree to their sending her away. But where? They couldn't let her reinfect Angie's family, who were still paying the price of offering her a home.

The children went to bed. The evening had a curious timeless quality about it, stretching endlessly in a dimension all its own. When she judged it had gone on long enough, Celia dragged herself upstairs to bed.

She dreamed, with almost photographic clarity, of Lucas Todd. She was out in a meadow with him in the very early morning and her feet were cold and wet with the heavy dew. There were huge columns of stone round about them—was it Stonehenge?—and in the distance she could see a circle of figures carrying torches and slowly gyrating. "Born in the bowels of the hills, evil ones, sowers of ills—"

Shuddering and gasping she forced herself awake, to find Tom's place beside her still empty. With a clutch of fear she switched on the light. Twelve o'clock. But the dance finished at ten. He must be back—or something had happened to him. In a panic she flung herself out of bed and ran out onto the landing. Downstairs the hall light which she had left on for them shone down on the hall table—and Eva's handbag. Eva's bag which, beyond shadow of doubt, she had taken with her this evening. So she at least was home. She would know where Tom was.

She turned and ran lightly, barefoot, up the four stairs leading to Eva's room, but at her first tap the door swung open. The room was in darkness, the bed empty. Thoroughly frightened now, Celia hurried across the landing and down

122

the stairs. In the hall she stood still, listening, but the only sound was the battering of her own heartbeats. Then, suddenly, from behind the study door came a creak and a rustle. She moved forward, twisted the handle and flung open the door.

Only one lamp was on, the one on Tom's desk, but its faint red glow illuminated the room sufficiently to reveal the figures of Tom and Eva together on the sofa. Celia's finger came down hard on the light switch and everything leapt into cruel clarity—Eva's dishevelled hair and unbuttoned blouse, the apprehension on Tom's face as he heaved himself off her.

He said thickly, "Celia, we weren't—it wasn't—" Then he swayed, clasped a hand to his mouth and lurched past her down the hall to the cloakroom. A moment later the stunned room rang to the retching and coughing of his vomiting.

Celia was icily calm. "You'd better go to your room," she told Eva. The girl nodded, her fingers deftly buttoning her blouse. Celia stood aside for her to pass and as she drew level Eva turned her head, paused for a moment and stared full into her eyes. Detachedly Celia tried with one part of her numbed brain to decipher the message. Pleasure? Triumph? Challenge? Or, more subtly, encouragement? But how, in these damning circumstances, could that be? Again a kind of spontaneous understanding interpreted for her. He has wronged you. Now there is nothing to hold you to him. You are free.

Free for what? For whom? Shivering more from reaction than cold, Celia switched off the lights and watched Eva go slowly up the stairs. A moment later, white-faced and shaking, Tom emerged from the cloakroom. He had at least the grace to look ashamed of himself.

"Celia, it wasn't as bad as it looked. It was—only a bit of fun."

She said coldly, "How did you manage to get so drunk at the dance?"

He flushed at her tone, the colour garish on his livid face. "We slipped out to the Coach and Horses from time to time. Hell's teeth, you didn't expect me to exist on orange squash, did you? Not tonight of all nights."

"I didn't expect you to slobber all over my sister, either."

"It was only the drink. Don't blame Eva—she tried to keep me at arm's length."

"Oh, I'm sure she did." With her full lips and dark eyes full of mysterious invitation. Wearily, beneath the sick disgust, she knew Tom was not to blame. If Eva had a doll in his image, complete with his own hair, what hope had he of withstanding her?

CHAPTER 10

THE next morning Tom was white and shaky and inclined to bluster his way out of the compromising situation in which he had been found. "I was worried sick about this drug business. Can you imagine how I felt, smiling and chatting to Colonel and Mrs. Hardacre, knowing what I'd have to tell them on Monday? All right, I know none of that is an excuse but at least it's a reason. A reason, anyway, why I let myself be convinced one more drink wouldn't do me any harm, or another, or another. Eva did drive home, by the way, which I can't help feeling was just as well. As for the rest, well, I was maudlin drunk and in the mood for a bit of petting. I'm not proud of my behaviour, but there's no need to make a Federal case out of it."

"I haven't said a word," Celia replied truthfully.

"You don't need to, I get the message. Okay, I'm sorry. Now can we forget it?"

"Are you going to apologize to Eva too?"

He flushed. "That wouldn't be exactly easy."

"True, since obviously she didn't object to what you were doing."

His colour deepened. "Oh, for heaven's sake, drop it. Leave me to sort things out. I'm trying to keep my mind clear

125

for Alan this morning and I feel pretty hellish, if that's any comfort."

Breakfast was a difficult meal, with the three of them striving for normality in front of the children. At least, Celia and Tom strove. Eva was her usual unforthcoming self. Tempers were not helped by the fact that Kate began one of her periodic demands for more pocket money.

"Everyone else has fifty pence," she complained in an aggrieved tone which, Celia realized wearily, was fast becoming her usual one.

"*If* anyone your age has fifty pence, which I doubt," Tom said heavily, "their parents are either irresponsible millionaires—and offhand I can't think of any millionaire's children at my school—or else they are expected to pay for their own clothes, sweets, bus fares and so on. You seem to forget we see to all those things."

"Jenny never pays for herself and *she* gets fifty pence."

"That's enough, Kate."

"But it's not *fair!*"

"I said that's enough!"

For a moment father and daughter glared belligerently at each other, their expressions almost identical. Then Tom pushed his chair back from the table and left the room.

"Daddy is *mean,*" Kate remarked to the room at large, surreptitiously achieving the satisfaction of the last word. Celia knew she should make some comment but her mind was blank and she let the remark go unchecked.

With Alan and Tom in the study and the heat switched off in the now-unused drawing-room, Celia spent the first half of the morning wandering round the kitchen, her mind seething with alternative courses of action. Kate had gone to Jenny's, no doubt seeking sympathy for her parents' parsimony, and Lucy had her nasty little dolls out again. One

126

looked much like another and Celia couldn't bring herself to ascertain whether her instructions had been carried out and the dolls representing real people removed. This negative attitude, however, triggered off a more positive one and she resolved to tackle Eva now, before her courage failed her. Leaving Lucy absorbed in her play she went out and closed the door quietly behind her. From the study came the sound of muted voices, low and grave.

Celia swung round the banisters and ran upstairs and up the little extra flight to Eva's door.

"Come in." She was sitting on the windowseat with the inevitable book. Celia's quick glance covered the entire room. There was nothing in sight which was at all out of place.

"Lucy tells me you have some obscene little dolls representing various members of the family. I'm afraid I must insist that you dispose of them immediately."

Eva smiled slightly. She closed her book and folded her hands over its smooth cover. "Certainly. How do you suggest I go about it?"

The swift capitulation was somehow not what Celia had expected. "I've no idea," she stammered. "Melt them down —burn them—anything."

"There's just one point I should mention," Eva said softly. "Whatever happens to the doll will happen to the person it represents."

Celia's brain reeled. "You admit, then, that they're voodoo dolls?"

"They're used for much the same purpose, yes."

"But *why*, Eva? What have we done that you should try to get your revenge in this horrible way?"

"The dolls, you mean? Actually I haven't used them yet. It hasn't been necessary. If you're referring to the episode last night, I just wanted to prove to you that Tom's not worthy of your loyalty."

"But you couldn't know that I'd come down."

"Of course I did. I woke you."

It didn't seem safe to pursue that line. Celia swallowed. "Tom has apologized. He explained he was drunk and it was all pretty innocent anyway."

Eva studied her nails. "All the same, I think it was as well that I woke you when I did. He was becoming increasingly hard to handle."

Celia felt her colour come and go while she battled with a fierce desire to slap the girl across her smug face. "All right," she said after a minute. "Why did you go to so much trouble to get Tom drunk and amorous when you apparently despise him so much?"

"I told you. To show you what he is. It was all in the cards but I didn't expect you to believe it. Now perhaps you do. You don't have to tie yourself to him any longer. You're destined for much greater things."

Again Celia's brain shied away from the unacceptable implications and she reverted to a marginally safer topic. "Can I see them?" she asked abruptly.

"The dolls? Of course." The girl uncurled from the window-seat, bent down and retrieved a flattish cardboard box from under the bed. "Help yourself." She dropped it carelessly onto the counterpane and turned away.

Tremblingly Celia lifted the lid. A row of some fifteen or so little dolls lay looking up at her, smiling emptily. A few were plastic or celluloid, the cheap kind sold in newsagents' and sweet shops, but their conventional clothes had been removed and odd pieces of cloth wrapped round them, held together with pins and elastic bands. With a shock Celia recognized a piece of material from her own housecoat, a scrap of one of Angie's summer dresses, something of Ruth's. A few of the dolls had a lifeless wad of presumably human hair fastened to their wax or plastic heads.

"You realize, of course," Eva remarked conversationally, "that I shall deny their existence."

"It wouldn't do you any good. Lucy has seen them."

"Lucy will deny it too."

Celia put a hand to her hot forehead. "You really believe that what you do to these dolls will happen to their originals?"

"More or less, yes. Of course the mommets as we call them are only symbols, a way of channelling concentration. The real force is in my mind. And yours—and Lucy's."

"But I really can't believe that if you dispose of them, harm will come to us."

"Are you prepared to risk it?" Eva asked calmly. "Personally I wouldn't, but it's up to you."

Distractedly Celia shook her head. "No, heaven help me, I'm not."

"Heaven won't help you," Eva said gently. "Hell might." She leant forward intently with clasped hands. "Why are you so stubborn and blind? You know what we want—you must. And it's so much to your own advantage I can't imagine why you even hesitate!"

" 'We?' " Celia's tongue was overlarge in her mouth and she had difficulty speaking. "You and Lucas Todd?"

Eva's small pointed face became transfigured with a kind of ecstasy. "You know who he is, though you won't even acknowledge him subconsciously. Tell me now! Admit it!" The intensity of her gaze numbed Celia's brain.

"Is he the leader of your—coven or something?"

"You always draw back, don't you?" Eva gave a light, excited laugh. "I don't belong to a coven but I suppose you're

129

on the right lines. He's certainly my leader, and he wants you. You and Lucy. And he'll get you eventually, of that I'm certain."

Fumblingly Celia dropped the lid on the rows of sinister smiling faces. "Please don't fill Lucy's head with any more nonsense."

"Lucy has an enquiring mind and a thirst for knowledge. What I don't tell her she'll find out for herself soon enough. She's a very adept pupil. It was because her powers were so promising that I arranged for the Master to come."

Celia said faintly, "He came in answer to Tom's advertizement."

Eva smiled placatingly. "Of course, of course. It must all seem perfectly natural. But who do you think arranged for Sue Carlton to start a baby a full year before she intended and so create a vacancy for a music teacher?"

"I don't believe it." But she did. Sue Carlton had become pregnant soon after Eva arrived at Angie's, and Eva had even then been interested in Lucy. "Anyway," she added challengingly, "if it wasn't by means of the advertizement, *how* did you arrange for him to come?"

Eva smiled. "So you do want to know? Good. That shows a much more positive approach. I called him. I explained how to Lucy and I'm quite prepared to tell you too."

"No!" Celia backed hurriedly away. "I don't want to hear."

"There are several ways of doing it, of course, but the best is acknowledged to be the rite of the 'dark ones of the Hungarian marshes'—in other words, Hungarian gypsies. If you remember, my mother was descended from them." The compelling voice went on, about churchyards and smoking bullrushes, and Celia was paralyzed, unable to turn, as she desperately wanted, and run from the room.

130

"And to thee, oh Prince of Darkness, my soul pays eternal homage. *Probatum, probatum, probatum.*"

Eva's breast was rising and falling with her rapid breathing and the light in her eyes inevitably made Celia think of madness. In the force of such total conviction, what chance had they? Her paralysis dissolved and she fled from the room, flinging herself on her bed in a storm of wild, terrified sobbing. Eva had followed her to the door of the room.

"Go to him," she said, "he is waiting for you. Nothing can be gained by delaying any further."

Celia flung her hands over her ears and continued to sob. The girl went away and soon afterwards the two men came out of the study. Down in the hall she heard Tom call her name. She was incapable of moving from the bed, unable anyway, red-eyed and blotchy as she was, to go downstairs. Tom came running up and she heard his indrawn breath as he saw her lying face down across the bed.

"Celia! Whatever is it? Honey, you're not still—?"

She swung round and caught hold of his hand, clinging tightly to it. "Send her away, Tom, now! She's evil! She means to destroy us all. She even has little dolls for sticking pins in!"

"Hey, hey, hey! What is all this? Look, I said I was sorry. There's no need to—"

"Tom, don't you *see*? It's not last night—or at least, that's only part of it. She thinks she can get at me by playing up to you, and you fell for it. But that's not the important thing. She's a witch, she—"

"There, there, darling, it's all right. It won't happen again, I promise. Just lie quietly and get your breath back while I see Alan off. He wanted to speak to you but I'll make some excuse. Then I'll bring you a glass of brandy and we'll talk things over calmly." He patted her hand and she heard him go downstairs and the murmur of voices in the hall. What was he saying? That she was neurotic, hysterical? It was useless, she thought hopelessly. Tom would never accept the enormity of what she had to tell him—but Alan might. He had sounded quite knowledgeable about the black arts at the birthday party.

Tom came back with the promised brandy, his eyes full of concern. He said contritely, "I didn't realize quite how upset you were. You seemed calm enough at the time."

She gave a noncommittal little shrug and held out her hand for the glass. There was no point in repeating her accusations against Eva. Tom in his male conceit was convinced his lapse was the cause of her breakdown. Instead she said shakily, "What did Alan say about the drugs?"

"Pretty much what I expected. The parents concerned will be asked to keep their children at home on Monday and to come to the school to see me at six o'clock. That will give the kids the chance to confess first if they want to. I'll have to call a meeting of the board of governors before I can take any definite action other than suspension till the end of term. It's only two weeks away, anyway."

"And does Alan think hard drugs are involved?"

"There's no proof of it. We can only hope."

"I think you should tell Angie and Michael first, privately."

"You can if you like. I'll have to keep it strictly impersonal. I can't show favouritism to the family, particularly since a large part of the blame is likely to be put on Ruth."

Celia took another gulp of brandy. "I don't think I could face them today. Perhaps tomorrow, when Mother's gone home after lunch."

As it happened, Ruth herself came that afternoon, her face white and frightened. Celia had only just time to pull her into

132

the kitchen and close the door before she burst into tears. Celia surveyed her helplessly. Her own paroxysm that morning had left her eyes swollen and her temples tender and Ruth's tears were an added strain.

"Sit down," she said quietly, "and tell me the truth. All of it."

"How much do you know?"

"I heard you were the one who started it. Is that true?"

She nodded miserably and blew her nose. "It was only supposed to be Pat and Daphne and me, but some of the boys found out and said they'd tell if we didn't let them have a go. And they passed it round and before we knew where we were there were about fifteen of us and I couldn't get enough stuff."

"Where did you get it from?" Ruth hesitated. "Come on. Unless I know it all I can't help you. I'm not sure that I can anyway."

"It was from Madame Stella."

"And I suppose Eva told you she could obtain it for you?"

"Not directly. I mean, it couldn't be traced back to Eva. She only hinted that was how Madame Stella managed her trance states and things. And she said how wonderful and clear and alive everything was when you were on a trip; how you saw all kinds of things that normally only sensitives can see, like Lucy and her coloured lights." She trembled suddenly. "She didn't say anything about the sickness and the —the terror."

"But even when you found out about that part, you went on with it?"

"I wanted to stop after the first time, even before the boys found out. But Pat and Daphne said we might as well at least finish the stuff we had, since we'd had to pay so much for it."

"Oh Ruthie, what *are* we going to tell your parents?"

Her eyes filled again. "They'll probably throw me out of the house."

"I doubt that. Does Martin know?"

"I don't think so. He heard me being sick once and I wondered if he suspected, but he never said anything. You know something? I shouldn't be surprised if Martin goes on with his theology after all."

"Oh?"

"He's a lot more serious these days. Now that Eva's out of his hair he might be all right in time."

"You never liked her, did you?"

"No, she was too sweet, too retiring. It was always the 'Who could possibly want poor little me?' act and a rather sick-making display of gratitude when anyone noticed her."

Celia smiled wryly. "Since you seem to have summed her up pretty accurately, I'm surprised you let her lead you astray."

"Yes, I was a fool. But you see, Daphne's always been my best friend. Pat only came to school at the end of last year when her family moved down here, but she cottoned on to Daphne and the two of them started to go around without me."

"So you wanted to establish yourself again."

"I suppose so. What's Uncle going to do about it?"

"He's seeing the parents on Monday evening, but he can't do much until the governors have had a chance to meet."

"Those old fogeys! They'll never understand."

"If I were you I should go home and tell your mother straight away. Break it to her as gently as you can, and be sure to make her understand that the whole experiment only made you feel rotten and you'll never have anything more to do with it."

"That's for sure, anyway."

134

"There wasn't any cocaine or morphia or anything, was there?"

"Lord, no."

"I hear a syringe was found."

"It would be Stewart's. He wanted to try 'mainlining.'"

"That sounds horribly professional."

"But it wasn't LSD or anything. He just split open the pep pills we had and put the powder in the syringe. He didn't even know where to prick himself and he was furious when he didn't get any results. I don't think he bothered again."

"Thank God for that. Well, I don't really see what I can do except keep my fingers crossed for you."

"You're all right yourself, aren't you, Auntie?"

"Yes, rather a nasty headache, that's all."

"I'm afraid this hasn't helped."

"Never mind. Would you like to stay and have some tea with us?"

"No, thanks. I couldn't face Uncle just now."

"You could have it in here with me."

Ruth smiled wanly. "No, really, thanks. I'd rather go home and get it all over with."

"All right. Good luck then."

So Eva was behind it, as she'd suspected. But as she'd also suspected, she had covered her tracks pretty well.

Sunday passed. On the surface things were unchanged. Eva still smiled her secret, downcast smiles, Kate and Lucy argued as usual, and Mrs. Bannerman was blandly unaware of gathering stormclouds. Celia's idea of enlisting Alan's help had crystallized to a firm resolve to see him on the Monday. In the meantime, she could only live through the intervening hours as best she could.

The next morning, therefore, when Tom and the girls had left for school and Eva for college, Celia made her way to

Alan's surgery and took her place in the waiting room. The receptionist greeted her with a smile.

"No appointment today, Mrs. Bannerman?"

"I'm afraid not. Could you slip me in when he has a moment free?"

"Of course." Within twenty minutes she was shown into Alan's surgery.

"Hello there! I must say I was surprised when Miss Denton said you were out there. What's the trouble?"

"It's not strictly medical, Alan, and I'll try not to take up too much of your time, but it's confidential and that's why I didn't want to see you at home."

"Okay. Shoot. I'm all ears."

"It mainly concerns Eva."

"Oh dear." He sat back, regarding her with a rueful smile. "I had a basin full of that from Angie not so long ago!"

"Did she tell you she blamed Eva for Martin turning down University and Ruth's O's?"

"Something like that."

"Well, I think she's right. I think she was directly responsible. I didn't take much notice at the time. Angie's always been one for passing the buck, but there's no doubt about it, Eva is certainly a troublemaker."

"I'm surprised to hear that from you. You were always her devoted slave."

"I know. That's what blinded me to it for a while."

"And what's she done this time?"

"For one thing, she's an extremely bad influence on Lucy."

"Lucy's a very strong-willed little girl. I'm surprised she's open to influence, good or bad."

"Also—" Celia hesitated. She was coming to the hard part and it was vitally important to convince him, to have him on

136

her side. "She seems to have some strange connection with Lucas Todd."

Alan raised an eyebrow. "Strange? How so?"

Celia laced her fingers tightly together and took the plunge, keeping her eyes down and speaking quickly. "She seems to think she's—some kind of a witch—" She hurried on, ignoring Alan's short, disbelieving laugh, "and she insists she got in touch with Lucas because she needed help in fostering Lucy's 'psychic powers.' "

"Ye gods and little fishes! And how was he supposed to help?"

"Alan, you'll find this hard to credit because I know you like him, but there's something very strange about him. He has a most uncanny power over people when he chooses to exercise it. Did Tom ever tell you about hearing him play the piano? It was almost like hypnosis. When you listen, all the finer edges of right and wrong become blurred. You find yourself thinking only of what you yourself want most in the world, and the easiest way of getting it."

"I remember you said something about not liking him the other week. You're surely not trying to tell me now that he's a witch too?"

"I rather think he's more than that."

"What?" He leant forward to catch her lowered voice.

"I said I think he's something more. Eva calls him 'the Master.' "

The amused incredulity left her brother's face. "Now wait a minute. Haven't you rather let your imagination run away with you? I quite appreciate that having Eva in the house has been a strain and I daresay she is rather an unusual girl, but all this talk of witches and evil influence—surely you must see how off-beam it is?"

"Oh Alan!" Tears rushed into her eyes. "I was counting

137

so much on you believing me! No one else will!"

"I'm hardly surprised. It seems rather obvious that you're more run down than you realize. You'll just have to take a hold on yourself, love."

"You heard Eva tell Tom's fortune—"

"Yes, it seems to be one of her party tricks. And a good job she made of it, too, though whether or not there's any truth in it we'll just have to wait and find out."

"But there is! Ever since that night, Tom's changed. He's become irritable and short-tempered and this drug business looks like finishing him. He seems to have lost all incentive, somehow. What was it she said? Something about his foundations crumbling, leaving him insecure. Well, he is! And she also said his emotional happiness was at a peak and he'd begin to be dissatisfied, and that seems to be happening too. We were perfectly happy before, but we've never had so many rows as—"

"Hey, hold on! You've obviously been bottling up things too long and they've got all out of proportion. You really must force yourself to be rational about it."

"How can I be rational when my family's threatened? Alan, the other day I was upstairs and Lucy 'willed' me to go down to her—and I did!"

"Come on now, she probably only said that to tease you."

"No, it was Kate who told me, and I certainly was very conscious of a strong pull to go down and find Lucy. And most horrible of all, Eva's teaching Lucy to make beastly little plasticine dolls and dress them up in things belonging to the family."

Alan frowned. "You're sure of this?"

"Of course I'm sure, I've seen them—Eva's as well. One with bits of Angie's blue dress tied on, and one with scraps of my housecoat. I'm *frightened,* don't you see? You seemed

138

to know so much about witchcraft when we talked that evening, I was sure you'd believe me. You *said* it was still prevalent."

"I was excepting present company! But let's get back to all that gibberish about Lucas."

"Eva said she called him up, by means of a spell."

"You don't believe that, surely?"

"I don't know what I believe, except that he's *evil*. There's no doubt about that, and Lucy adores him. That's what terrifies me. And she insists that when he stares into her eyes she knows she can do anything she wants to—play the piano so beautifully, for instance. She's only—"

"Slow down a minute, you keep losing me!"

"I told you before about how well she plays, and she never practices at all. And I also told you she says Lucas has no aura."

"Ah yes, the mystic aura. But with all due respect, we don't *know* that's what Lucy's talking about. I just jumped to that conclusion because it seemed to fit, but if she says Lucas hasn't one obviously it can't be, since all living things have. You must remember that I haven't discussed it with her, or tried to find out exactly what form this light that she sees takes. It may quite simply be something she just pretends about. Now don't argue, love. Just collect yourself and tell me what you *definitely* have against Eva and Lucas. I'm afraid impressions, however strong, just won't do."

"Well, Eva said——"

"Sorry, no go. We can't necessarily believe what she said. Only concrete evidence is watertight. These dolls, for instance. Where does she keep them?"

"Under her bed."

"Then I suggest I call at the house unexpectedly and ask to see them."

"Oh Alan, would you? Lucy's seen them too—that's what started her off on hers."

"Well, I should certainly discourage that. It seems unhealthy, to say the least. Now, what else?"

"She frightens the children with talk of spirits and witches. Kate woke screaming one night."

"I'm afraid that won't do either. You've told them stories about witches yourself. What about *Snow White* and *Hansel and Gretel*? They always scared the daylights out of me when I was young. I sympathize with Kate, but we can hardly slate Eva for that."

"But her witches were *real*. At least, she said they were."

"Hearsay evidence again. She was probably only trying to make the story come alive. It looks as though all we have are the dolls. I suppose we could tax her with those, but I don't know where we'd go from there. At a pinch we might get her for intimidation, but only if she's actually threatened someone with them. And what about Lucas? You can hardly make a case against him that Lucy has done remarkably well in her lessons and his music makes you feel funny."

"He sucked my finger," Celia said woodenly.

"He *what*?"

"Sucked my finger. The one with the little lump."

"Why on earth?"

"I don't know."

"Well, whatever turns you on! Though if he's given to that kind of thing I should take care you're never alone with him, nor Lucy either. Let me have a look at that finger."

She held it out and he examined it, moving her hand round to see it from all angles.

"It seems to have turned into quite a nasty little wart."

"Is that what it is? Lucy has one on the same finger."

"I could give you some ointment but I can't guarantee it'll

140

work." He smiled a little ruefully. "Ask Eva's help! Warts are notoriously susceptible to spells!"

"In other words you think I'm making a fuss about nothing."

"I think you're thoroughly run down and have let things get on top of you. I'll write you a prescription for a tonic. Are you sleeping all right?"

She couldn't tell him about those shatteringly detailed dreams. "Reasonably."

"I could give you a sedative to take an hour before you go to bed. It might calm you down a bit. And I'll try to drop in during the next day or two and have a word with Eva about her dolls."

"And Lucas?"

"Sweetie, you've *nothing* on him. Nothing. Can't you see that?" He hesitated. "Is it possible that perhaps against your will you find him attractive?"

She flushed hotly. "I loathe him!"

"That wasn't the question. I don't doubt that you loathe him. I'm only saying *perhaps,* subconsciously, there's some basic attraction and your conscience has obligingly transformed the underlying guilt into a fantasy about evil influence and all the rest of it."

"Very plausible," she said tightly.

"Well, it's only a tentative theory. Psychology's not my line. As to his connection with Eva, short of seeing her conjuring him up in a cloud of smoke, I positively refuse to believe that there's anything sinister between them. I'm quite prepared to grant you that Eva's a nasty little piece of goods. I never liked her mother either, but that's another story. Filial jealousy, I suppose. But when you come down to brass tacks there's nothing to connect her with Lucas other than normal teenage admiration which, according to Tom, is

141

pretty widespread." He paused, studying her averted face. "I've a feeling I haven't been much help."

"I admit I'd hoped for more, especially since you acknowledged the existence of supernatural powers."

"In theory, yes. It's rather different when you're tied down to specific cases, particularly when it concerns your own stepsister!"

"All right. Thanks for hearing me out, anyway. I suppose it helped a bit."

"You won't agree that it could be because you're somewhat overwrought?"

"I only wish it was." She stood up. "Anyway, what I've said is confidential. If this visit is mentioned at all, it was only the sedatives I wanted."

"All right. Though it mightn't be a bad idea to confide in old Tom."

"Tom," she said in a low voice, "is the last person I could confide in at the moment. Especially about Eva."

"Oh?" Alan waited but she was walking to the door.

"Love to Melanie and Robert when you write. How's he getting on?"

"Oh, buried up to the elbows in entrails and loving every minute of it!"

She made a little grimace. "As you said, whatever turns you on!"

The door closed behind her. For a moment Alan sat staring at it with a slight frown. Then he reached forward and pressed the buzzer for the next patient.

CHAPTER 11

Tom's meeting with the parents that evening was obviously a considerable strain. He arrived home looking drawn and helped himself to a liberal measure of whisky. "God, I feel foul! I wouldn't go through that again for a million pounds."

"Did you gather the children had paved the way?" Celia enquired.

"Most of them, yes. Ruth certainly had. Actually, there was less hostility than I'd anticipated. They were obviously in a state of shock, poor devils. They agreed meekly to keeping the kids at home till we can reach some official decision. Personally I'm hoping that the two-week suspension will be enough. They've learned their lesson. I doubt if they'll mess about with anything like that again. Our main concern is trying to keep it out of the press, which won't be easy."

He poured another drink. Celia watched him anxiously but dared make no comment. "I think I'll take a couple of aspirins and go to bed. I've had quite enough of today."

But he did not sleep well. Through her own troubled dreams, Celia was aware of his tossing and turning. At one point he even got out of bed and stood looking out of the window for several minutes. The next morning found them both pale and heavy-eyed.

Mindful of Lucas's criticism, Celia asked Tom to leave her the car and phoned Mrs. Bannerman to offer her a lift to the shops. It appeared, however, that she had been forestalled. She was informed with some satisfaction that Lucas had called the day before, after Celia had gone out, and had been only too pleased to run her to the High Street. Celia found herself automatically apologizing. "I'm sorry, but actually I didn't go shopping myself yesterday. I had to go—to a meeting."

"Oh, it's quite all right, dear. You know I don't like to be any trouble."

With temper held carefully in check, Celia left the car in the garage and walked down through the park. She had finished shopping and was crossing the High Street on her way home when she was startled to catch a sudden glimpse of Kate among the crowds on the pavement. She called out and started to hurry toward her, but the street was thronged with Christmas shoppers and by the time she reached the spot, Kate, if it had indeed been Kate, had disappeared.

Celia was faintly uneasy. It was eleven-thirty. Kate should, of course, be at school. It was possible that the class had been on some educational outing by train, but if so it hadn't been mentioned at breakfast, nor could Celia remember having been asked to pay for it.

When taxed with the question on her return that afternoon, Kate categorically denied that she had been in the High Street at all that day. "How could I possibly?" she kept repeating. "I was at school!"

Celia was still sufficiently doubtful to ask Tom to check if the child had been marked absent. When he reported that her name was ticked in the register as being present, she had no course but to put the incident out of her mind. Obviously it couldn't have been Kate that she had seen after all.

144

As promised, Alan dropped in on his way home on the evening after Celia's visit. He accepted Tom's offer of a drink and settled back in one of the deep leather chairs, watching him as he moved to the cabinet.

"You don't look too hot, lad. Not in for a dose of flu, are you?"

"I hope not. As a matter of fact I've felt pretty groggy ever since the weekend. It's probably just the usual buildup of pressure at the end of term, and of course that other business didn't help."

"You ought to relax more, you know. Ever thought of joining the golf club?"

Tom pulled a face and handed him his glass. "Can't afford it."

"Well, take up some hobby completely unconnected with teaching: philately, for instance. The collecting bug can become very absorbing. It's quite amazing the things people collect—matchboxes, cardboard drinks mats, buttons. I believe you have a collection of dolls, Eva?"

Celia held her breath. She hadn't realized the direction the casual conversation was taking.

Eva looked up in surprise. "Dolls? I'm afraid I grew out of dolls some time ago!"

"But I understood these were rather special. More—collectors' items?"

She shook her head. "Sorry, not me. You must be thinking of someone else. Dolls were never much in my line anyway. I always preferred teddy-bears, didn't I, Celia?"

Celia smiled vaguely and glanced at Alan, who met her eye with a resigned little shrug. She said quickly, "Alan's probably thinking of the ones you have under your bed."

Eva stared at her blankly. "Under my bed? Whatever are you talking about?" *I shall deny their existence, of course.*

145

Coldness crept along Celia's neck and inched up into her scalp. "The ones you showed me the other day," she persevered without hope, "in the cardboard box."

Eva looked from one of them to the other. "Is this some kind of joke? I don't understand."

"Lucy!" Celia's voice shook and the child, busy with paper and crayons at the far end of the room, looked round. "Do you remember telling me about Eva's dolls, and how she bought you plasticine to make some of your own?"

Lucy frowned. "Dolls? Like Ruby, do you mean?"

Icy sweat drenched Celia's body. "No," she said sharply, "not like Ruby. Like me and Daddy and Auntie Angie. You said you were making the school."

There was a pause. "I made a school out of bricks during the holidays," Lucy volunteered helpfully.

"What is all this?" Tom demanded. "Will someone tell me what you're all going on about?"

"Perhaps there's been some mistake—" Eva murmured.

Celia stood up abruptly. "There's no mistake. Do you deny the box is under your bed?"

Eva smiled with just the right amount of patient bewilderment. "Of course I deny it! What box? I simply don't know what you're talking about."

"Then may we go up to your room now and look for ourselves?"

"I wish you would!"

They all trooped up the stairs, but Celia already knew that the girl's calm confidence could only mean that the dolls had been removed. It was the fact that *Lucy* had denied all knowledge of them—

The space under the neat single bed was bare.

"Lucy's will still be in the toy-box, at any rate." Celia

raced back down the stairs, dropping to her knees to pull out the battered box and scrabbling frantically among paint boxes, books and jigsaw puzzles. No plasticine was in sight and certainly no macabre little figures. Celia sat back on her heels and looked up, seeing the doubt on her brother's face as he followed her into the room.

"Did Celia tell you Eva had dolls of some sort?" Tom demanded.

Alan hesitated, aware of his promise of secrecy.

"Yes, I did," Celia said clearly.

"I'm damned if I see what's so important about them."

"They were voodoo dolls, made in our likenesses."

Tom flushed darkly. "You went running to Alan with a story like that? Don't you think it was rather unnecessary?"

"No, I don't. They were revolting, a horrible, sordid—"

"Sordid, yes—that's the key word." Tom's voice was harsh. He turned heavily to Alan. "I'm sorry you've been dragged into this. I'm afraid there's a perfectly simple explanation. I had too much to drink at the school dance on Friday—mainly because of worry about the dope—and Celia came downstairs to find Eva and me fooling about a bit. I thought she'd accepted my apologies but obviously some involved sort of revenge was necessary."

"That's a horrible thing to say," Celia protested in a low voice.

"Do you deny that when Alan was here on Saturday you were having hysterics on the bed and refused to come down and see him?"

Alan said gently, "Don't talk to her like that, old boy. She certainly gave me the impression of believing what she told me."

"She's moved them, that's all!" Celia insisted with rising

147

desperation. "She warned me she'd deny all knowledge of them, and Lucy's sufficiently under her thumb to say what she's been told."

"So everyone's lying except you?" Tom suggested sarcastically, looking meaningly at his brother-in-law. To her horror, Celia burst into tears. Alan came forward quickly and helped her to her feet.

"Come on, honey, it's all right."

"When did she spin you this tale? Did she go to see you?"

"Yes, at the surgery."

"Believe me, that's the right place for her. She's sick all right. Did she tell you about finding me with Eva?"

"No," Alan answered quietly.

"There you are. She couldn't bear to admit to it so she dressed it all up in a substitute accusation against Eva."

Hopelessly Celia turned and left them. No one would believe her. Eva and Lucas had already alienated her husband and daughter. She could see that even Alan was seriously doubting the existence of the dolls. Obviously Lucy's convincing innocence had swung the balance. And he had warned her that the dolls were the only concrete thing she had to back her admittedly wild accusations. For one reason or another they were now all arrayed against her. She was totally alone.

That evening was the first time Celia acknowledged to herself the extent of her helplessness. To protest any more, about either Eva or Lucas, would merely add to the family's suspicion that she was becoming unbalanced. She saw now that it had been a mistake not to have told Alan about Tom and Eva, but could he really believe that the torrent of suspicion she had poured out to him had been a pathetic attempt at revenge? He had already produced a plausible explanation for her tirade against Lucas: subconscious guilt because she

148

was unwillingly attracted by him. That, she thought wearily, was the most nauseating part of it. She *was* attracted to him, as they all were in varying degrees. It was his power of attraction which was the most dangerous thing about him. And Lucy's music lesson was due.

Her daughter's betrayal had upset Celia more than anything else. Although she admitted the strength of Eva's influence, she found it hard to forgive Lucy for letting her down so badly in her moment of need. The atmosphere between them was strained, as, Celia thought despairingly, was that between herself and Tom—and Eva—and even Alan. It was in total silence that they drove through the dark wet streets to the flat in Front Street.

Normally on these occasions, Lucas's attention was focused on his pupil but this evening he left her playing a piece by Chopin and came across to where Celia lay back against the cushions, drained and vulnerable. He sat on the edge of the sofa beside her, studying her face intently. "Look at me, Celia."

She had no strength to resist. Mindlessly she moved her head, experiencing a tremor of shock as her eyes encountered the force in his. Minute after long minute they sat motionless, their gaze interlocked, and gradually her despair and hopelessness began to disperse like the clearing of a thick grey fog. After all, what was to be gained by fighting them all? She couldn't convince them of her fears. No one could say she hadn't tried to warn them—they simply wouldn't listen. She might just as well relax and let events take their course. Oh, the relief it would be to stop worrying! And, on reflection, just what was she worrying about? If Tom found Eva attractive, did it really matter? The Tom she had known and loved for so long had been replaced by a pale, irritable stranger. Or perhaps this was the real Tom emerging at last.

Eva and Lucas knew him for what he was, and despised him.

As for Lucy, no harm had come to her. Far from it, she was now a brilliantly accomplished pianist. And if, as seemed likely, Eva had blotted the memory of the dolls from her mind, the child had not knowingly hurt her.

Celia's eyelids began to feel heavy. She had not been sleeping well, nor had she bothered to collect Alan's prescription. She gave Lucas a dazed little smile and closed her eyes. Sleep was instant, total and restoring. When at last she stirred, more than an hour had passed, the lesson was over and Lucas himself was at the piano.

The addictive music seeped lethally into her body and brain, drenching her with its heady excitement. How powerful he was, how wonderful and exciting and how different from tired, peevish Tom! And how he had bent them all to his will: Tom and Lucy, Mrs. Bannerman and Angie, Frances Delamere and the girls at school, Alan and Eva—all of them to some extent admired, loved or worshipped him. Yet Eva had told her it was she he wanted, she and Lucy. Why? There was no knowing, but she was aware of pride and gratification.

She realized that although she had not moved and he hadn't turned his head, he knew she was awake and wanted her to go to him. Like a sleepwalker she rose to her feet and moved across the room. She stopped behind him, staring down at the dark, springing hair, the narrow shoulders and the long, sensitive fingers which seemed to flow effortlessly over the keys as the music pulsated in her head.

Gently she rested her hands on his shoulders, jerking violently as a strong current flowed from his body into her own. There's nothing I can't do! she told herself exultantly, and dimly recognized in the thought an echo of Lucy.

The music stopped. He reached for her hand and pulled

150

it avidly down to his mouth. This time there was no revulsion, only contented acceptance. With her free hand she caressed the bent head, the line of his jaw curiously smooth to her fingers as it had been in her dream. After a while he raised his head and turned to look up into her face. What he saw there must have satisfied him, for he smiled slowly and, still with her hand in his, rose to his feet. From the doorway Lucy's voice said petulantly, "Mummy, I'm hungry. When are we going home? It's long past supper time."

Lucas laughed. "So it is, my little witch, so it is! Your mother has been resting but she will come with you now." He gave Celia a mock bow, raised her hand formally to his lips and she again felt the swift flick of his tongue on her throbbing finger. Lucy had gone into the hall to collect her coat. "When will you come?" he asked softly, "Tomorrow?"

She shook her head, unable to speak.

"Soon, Celia, soon. I've been very patient."

She smiled at him vaguely, took Lucy's hand and stumbled with her down the stairs. The night air struck her face like a douche of cold water, making her gasp. What had been happening while she was in that peculiar trance? She had only the dimmest remembrance of the last two hours. Lucy said in a whine, "Mummy! Open the door! I'm cold."

Her hands were shaking so much it took several attempts to insert the car key. Inside the dark cavern she gripped the steering wheel convulsively. "I think I must have fallen asleep, dear. How long ago did your lesson finish?"

"Ages ago. Mr. Todd wouldn't let me wake you. When I got bored of hearing him play, I went to his kitchen to look for something to eat but I couldn't find anything. His recipe books aren't like yours. They're all spelt wrong."

The clock on the dashboard said half-past seven. Tom would be wondering where they were. Closing her mind to everything but driving, she started up the engine.

Tom was up in the bedroom changing when they reached home. "It's about time you came! Where the hell have you been? Had you forgotten it's the carol concert?"

"Oh Tom, I'm so sorry. I fell asleep."

His eyes raked her face, suspicious and hostile. "In his bed?"

She said quietly, "Don't be ridiculous."

He looked away. "Anyway, I couldn't wait for you. Eva cooked me something. I wasn't really hungry but she said I had to eat."

"So you must." Achingly she studied the drawn, unhappy face. "Oh Tom, do you have to go out tonight? You look so tired."

"Of course I have to. I think Alan must have been right about the flu, though. I feel rotten. And where's my blue shirt, by the way? It's not in my drawer."

"It should be. I washed it last week."

"I know it *should* be but it damn well isn't. It's not asking much, surely, to be able to find a clean shirt once in a while?"

Calmly, closing her ears to his ranting, she looked methodically first in his chest of drawers, then in the airing cupboard and finally in the laundry basket. There was no sign of the missing shirt.

"What did I tell you? Well, leave it for now. You'd better hurry. Aren't you going to change?"

"I? Oh Tom, I can't! I haven't had anything to eat and I must get the children's meal."

"You're coming, my girl, whether you like it or not. You weren't at the dance and people will start talking, especially if they find out the amount of time you spend at Lucas's flat."

"Oh Tom!" she cried, "What's happening to us? We never used to quarrel like this."

152

He stared at her truculently. "I had a filthy headache when I came home and you weren't even here. It was Eva who had to massage it for me and get me something to eat. It's all very well for you to throw hysterics every time I look at her, but you bring it on yourself. If you'd come to the dance with me, or been home this evening—"

"Darling, I'm sorry. I was jealous, I admit it. Please don't be angry any more."

"Well all right, forget it." He stood woodenly while she reached up to kiss him and gave her arm a perfunctory pat. "Come on now, we'll have to go. I said we'd meet the vicar at eight."

"The vicar?"

"Oh wake up, for goodness sake! You know he always comes to the carol concert."

"It's about the only time we ever see him."

"He took the service for Frances."

Frances. Frances Delamere, running in tears from Lucas's flat. Incredibly Celia had almost forgotten her. It might have been better if she herself had run, rather than lie back and let the sweet, honeyed poison flow over her. What had he said as she was leaving? "When will you come? I've been very patient." Had she committed herself to him in some way? Had she signed away her soul as Tom had so casually three months ago?

She allowed him to hurry her out to the car again and once more they were going down the dark glistening streets. The vicar and his wife were waiting for them. They all went in together and the school rose in a body to welcome them. Then the lights went down and the children, solemn-faced, began their concert.

"God rest you merry, gentlemen, let nothing you dismay. Remember Christ our Saviour was born on Christmas

Day, to save us all from Satan's power when we are gone astray—"

She was not actually aware of crying, only of the continuous and embarrassing tears streaming down her face. The vicar leant towards her. "If I can be of any help, Mrs. Bannerman—?"

Helplessly she shook her head. The unbearable nostalgia of all the well-known words pierced her with a special poignancy and beneath it her tortured mind writhed with queries as to what had really happened on Front Street earlier that evening. *To save us all from Satan's power—*

At last the kindly Mr. Simpson leant across her and touched Tom's arm. "Mr. Bannerman, I'm afraid your wife isn't well. I feel perhaps you should take her home."

Tom said expressionlessly, "Yes, you're right. If you'll excuse me—"

"Of course, of course."

The car again, and Tom silent at her side. Only as they turned into their own driveway was she able to speak. "I'm sorry," she said with difficulty.

"It's all right. Actually I thought I was going to pass out myself."

He opened the front door and stood aside for her to go in. There was a light in the study and Eva came to her feet, surprised at their early return.

Tom said, "Celia didn't—" and swayed suddenly, clutching his chest. Clumsily Celia tried to move toward him, but Eva was there before her, supporting his weight and easing him down onto the sofa. Frantically Celia dropped to her knees beside him, registering his colourless face and closed lids with terror. "Ring Alan, Eva! Quickly!"

154

"It's all right, the spasm's past." Eva looked at her intently. "Is there anything I can get you?"

"Me? No, we must look after Tom."

"Tom's fine." There was a touch of impatience in her voice.

His eyelids fluttered. "Eva?"

"I'm here, Tom."

Fumblingly his hand moved and she closed hers over it. Celia said with an effort, "It's all right, thank you, Eva, I'll see to him."

"You have more important things to do," she answered in a low voice. "It's still only nine-thirty. Go now—he'll be waiting. I'll distract Tom."

Celia bent forward and pushed the girl's hand off Tom's. "Leave him alone! Do you hear me?"

Eva said in a low, vicious undertone, "Oh, you fool! Are you still resisting? Don't you see that there's nothing else left for you now?"

Tom's eyes opened suddenly and stared blankly up at them.

"Help me get him to bed," Celia commanded. For a moment Eva's lips tightened and it seemed she would refuse. Then, with a resigned shrug, she bent down and slid an arm under Tom's heavy, limp body. Between them they pulled him to his feet and slowly, inch by inch, across the hall and up the stairs. On the landing, barefoot and in her nightdress, Lucy surveyed their erratic progress.

"Is Daddy ill?" she asked without interest. They had no breath to answer her and after a moment she turned and padded back to bed. As they reached their own room Tom raised his head.

155

"Thanks. I'm all right now. What happened?"

Above his head, Celia's eyes found Eva's. She knows, she thought with certainty. She knows exactly what happened. As though reading her mind, the girl smiled slightly and left them. Wearily Celia began to help Tom to undress.

CHAPTER 12

IT was obvious the next morning that Tom was not well enough to go to school. Celia phoned Alan at home before breakfast and explained what had happened and he promised to call on his way to the surgery. Rather to her surprise, Tom had not protested when she suggested he should stay in bed and this in itself alarmed her. Normally he insisted on getting up and had been known to stagger downstairs with a temperature of a hundred and three degrees. Nor was she reassured by Alan's visit. He gave Tom a thorough examination, including checking his blood pressure, but confessed to Celia that he was not sure what was wrong.

"It might well be just a slant on the old flu virus," he told her. "His skin is dry and burning but he doesn't complain of any specific symptoms. This new antibiotic is working wonders—two tablets every four hours. Send Eva to the chemist with the prescription as soon as they open." He looked at her closely. "Did the pills I gave you help at all?"

"I'm all right," she said evasively.

"You haven't taken them, have you?"

She shook her head and he sighed. "I can't force you. I'll call in tomorrow morning and see how Tom is. There should be a marked improvement by then."

157

Celia went to the chemist herself. She no longer trusted Eva. Suppose she tampered with the pills in some way? It was an illogical fear, as she knew only too well. Eva did not need such concrete things as pills to do harm. When she reached home again, Tom lay listlessly in the same position as she had left him. He swallowed the pills obediently and made no objection when she suggested he should try to sleep.

She closed the bedroom door softly and paused on the landing. Eva had gone to college, the children to school. There was some washing she should do. It was strange about Tom's missing shirt. Frowningly she remembered that a week or two ago he had mislaid a vest which had never reappeared. Her eyes swivelled almost fearfully to the bland face of Eva's closed door. There was no reason to suppose that Eva knew anything about Tom's clothes other than a growing certainty that she was behind any mystery, however slight. With a feeling of guilt, Celia went up the steps. She was still sure that a thorough search of the room would reveal the missing box of dolls, and she told herself that she owed it to her family and herself to find them. Even so, the seeming necessity to search through the girl's things was distasteful to her.

The box of candles was still in its hiding place in the bottom drawer but there were only four candles left in it. Sickly, Celia wondered how the others had been used. The wardrobe and the other drawers, in dressing table and dresser, revealed nothing untoward. Defeated, she stood in the center of the room, wondering where else she could look. Eva's suitcase was on top of the wardrobe. It was a forlorn hope, but Celia dragged a chair over and climbed up to lift it down. It was unlocked and inside, under layers of tissue paper, was, unbelievably, a neat pile of Tom's clothes: the missing blue shirt, a vest, pants, socks. A feeling of vindica-

158

tion underlay her amazement; the surreptitious search had not been in vain after all. Would Eva notice if she removed the clothes? She picked them up and as she did so a piece of paper hidden in the folds of the shirt fluttered to the ground. She bent quickly and picked it up.

"Gain possession of some garments of the man," she read incredulously. "Wash and press them and make them fair—"

With a little gasp she crumpled the paper in her hand and laid the clothes on the bed while she replaced the suitcase on top of the wardrobe. Tom was asleep when she returned to their room. She opened his drawers quietly and put away the clothes, then she went downstairs, the paper still in her hand. She spread it out on the kitchen table and read it again. That it was a spell of some kind she had no doubt. Would this convince Alan that her accusations were not unfounded?

"Celia?"

She spun round, stuffing the paper into the pocket of her skirt. "Yes, in the kitchen."

Angie came into the room and dropped down onto one of the chairs. "Coffee, for the love of Allah!"

"Of course. Angie, I meant to phone you but things have been so frantic this week."

"It's all right. There wasn't much you could have said. Ruth told me she'd been to see you."

"I'm so terribly sorry about it all."

"What's Tom going to do, do you know?"

"He's hoping the governors will agree that the two-week suspension will be enough."

"I hope he pulls it off. Ruth's moping round the house like a lost soul. Surprisingly enough though, Martin's being very good with her. It's the first time in over a year that they've spent any time together without swearing at each other."

"Perhaps Eva's influence is wearing off."

Angie smiled a little self-consciously. "I admit I got a bit steamed up about Eva, but it really did seem as though everything that went wrong dated from her arrival."

"I'm sure you were right. The same thing's happening here."

"Really? Why, what's wrong?"

"She plays up to Tom, for one thing. By the way, he's in bed. He's not at all well. Alan was here this morning."

"Oh, I'm sorry. Flu?"

"He doesn't seem to know what it is. Then Kate's being difficult and sulky and Mother's awkward—but that's more Lucas's fault than Eva's."

"The rather gorgeous Mr. Todd? What's he got to do with it? That reminds me, I was going to ask you: I've only met him a couple of times, but do you think I could invite him round for drinks at Christmas? An attractive unattached man is always an asset."

"I shouldn't let him inside the house if I were you." Celia shuddered, spilling the coffee in her saucer. "He's deadly, Angie, and so's Eva. As I said, you were right about her, but you didn't know the half of it. She actually has some disgusting little dolls dressed up in scraps of our clothes."

Angie stared at her unbelievingly. "Oh come on, Celia, you must be making it up!"

"I'm not, believe me. And didn't Ruth tell you it was Eva who steered her to Madame Stella for the drugs?" She felt in her pocket, and produced the crumpled piece of paper. "She had some things of Tom's in her suitcase and this was among them. Read it!"

"Things of Tom's? What on earth—?"

"Read the paper!"

Angie ran her eye down it. "What is it?"

"A spell of some sort, obviously."

160

"A *spell*? My dear Celia, you can't be serious!"

"I've never been more so. Do you know what she told me? That she called up Lucas—she calls him the Master—to help her train Lucy."

"Called him up?" Angie echoed faintly.

"Yes. She worships him. Quite literally. She's a kind of—devil's disciple."

"Meaning that *Lucas* is—?" Angie was staring at her as though she doubted her hearing. She laughed shakily. "Good grief, Celia, you almost had me going then! What's the idea —a kind of December April Fools' Day?"

"Remember the teacher from the school who committed suicide? She was at his flat. I saw her."

"Then so were you, presumably. What possible connection is there?"

"She went back there the night she died. She killed herself because she found out who he really was and she'd fallen in love with him."

Angie said, "For pity's sake give me a cigarette."

Celia reached behind her for a packet Tom had left on the dresser. "For some reason he's trying to get hold of me."

"Lucky you! Tell him I'm willing to risk being caught!"

"You don't know what you're saying."

"And nor, my love, do you. How on earth did you dream up all this rubbish? You can't have the smallest shred of evidence."

"I haven't," she admitted in a low voice. "They're too clever for that. At least—I have that paper—" Wildly she looked round. "Where is it? That piece I gave you?"

Angie picked up her handbag and looked underneath it, and simultaneously their eyes fastened on the charred remnants in the ashtray. "Oh Celia, I'm sorry. Did you want it back? I must have used it as a spill for my cigarette."

161

Celia said dully, "It doesn't matter. I should have known I wouldn't be allowed to keep it."

Angie leant forward. "Look, *I* burned it. I'm sorry, it was an accident, but I did it of my own free will and no supernatural power made me."

"It has to *appear* normal. That's what Eva said about arranging for Lucas to come. She fixed it so that Sue Carlton would have her baby a year earlier than she'd planned." She avoided her sister's dumbfounded eyes. "All right, I know it sounds insane but it just happens to be true."

Angie moistened her lips. "Have you spoken to anyone else about these—these fantasies?"

"I told Alan."

"What did he say?"

"That I need concrete evidence. We arranged for him to come and see the wax dolls but of course she'd moved them."

Out in the hall the telephone shrilled suddenly and Celia moved heavily to answer it.

"Mrs. Bannerman? I'm sorry to trouble you but is your husband available? I phoned the school and was told he's not in today."

"I'm afraid he isn't well. I'd rather not disturb him, if you don't mind. Who's speaking?"

"My name is York, of Rawdons Department Store."

"Perhaps I can help you?"

"Unfortunately it's rather a delicate matter. It involves your daughter Katherine. I do feel that either you or your husband should be here."

"Kate?" Celia's voice clogged in her throat. "What is it? Has she been hurt? What's happened?"

"She's not hurt, no, but I'm sorry to have to tell you that she and some friends were stopped leaving the premises with goods they hadn't paid for."

162

"There must be some mistake." Her voice was hardly above a whisper.

"I beg your pardon?"

"I said there must be some mistake."

"It appears not. I rather gather this isn't the first occasion."

"Is she there with you now?"

"Yes, she's in my office. The police have had to be informed, of course."

Celia said expressionlessly, "I'll be there in ten minutes."

Angie was still at the kitchen table, staring unseeingly into her coffee cup. Celia said, "Will you come with me to Rawdons? They've got Kate there. Apparently they're accusing her of shoplifting."

"*What?*"

"Will you come, Angie?" Celia's voice rocked. "I can't worry Tom with it."

"Of course I'll come. My car's outside—we'll go in that."

As they drove down Regent's Walk, Angie said bracingly, "I shouldn't worry, it's probably a case of mistaken identity or something."

"I doubt it. I thought I saw her in the High Street the other day but she denied being there. How she manages to get in and out of school whenever she feels like it without anyone noticing I just don't understand. She's marked 'present' on the register."

"She probably slips out later. I believe that's what happens in a lot of schools."

"But *why*, Angie? Whatever possessed her to do this?"

They parked in the carpark behind the store and a serious-faced assistant took them up the stairs to the manager's office. Celia nodded to the two frightened-looking women beside the desk, one of whom she recognized as Jenny Dexter's mother. Then Jack Barlow, the deputy head of the school, hurried forward to greet her. "Mrs. Bannerman, I don't know what to say."

Kate and Jenny and a child Celia didn't know were lined up against one wall. On the desk was a motley collection of items: powder compacts, some costume jewelry, a bottle of After Shave. The manager gravely introduced them to the police sergeant and the store detective. Apparently the store had been concerned for some months about the increase in shoplifting and the children had aroused suspicion because they should have been in school. Mechanically Celia answered the questions put to her. She was duly advised that she would be kept informed of proceedings and the children, defiant and frightened, were taken back to school by the grim-faced Jack Barlow.

Back in the car Celia said dully, "Now do you believe me? One after another we're all succumbing."

"You blame Eva for Kate's shoplifting?"

"It's just the gradual eroding of moral standards: Martin dropping out, Ruth taking drugs, Tom drinking too much, and now Kate."

"Celia, you must pull yourself together. You're becoming obsessed by all this."

"Do you blame me?"

Angie drew up outside the house. "I don't like leaving you, but Michael's bringing a client home for lunch."

"It doesn't matter."

"Celia, promise me you won't think any more about all the ludicrous things you were saying before."

"You don't believe me?"

"How can I possibly? Give Tom my love. I hope he's better soon."

"So do I. What I have to tell him won't help."

But Tom did not appear interested in his daughter's mis-
demeanour. In fact, Celia was doubtful whether he even
heard, though his eyes were fixed on her face throughout her
recital.

"We'll just have to wait and see what action they propose
to take," she finished. He nodded absently. "How do you
feel?"

"Much the same."

"It's time for more pills." She handed him a glass of water.
The heat from his body reached her through his pyjama
jacket as she supported his back while he drank. "I have to
slip out for a while this afternoon. Will you be all right?"

"Yes, I shan't be wanting anything."

The skin on his face seemed to hang loosely, as though the
flesh beneath it had withered away. His eyes looked hollow
and black-rimmed. Perhaps after the second dose of pills he
would begin to improve.

She stood at the kitchen table to drink her coffee, the only
lunch she wanted. Sometime during the morning, after Angie's failure to understand, a plan had occurred to her. It was
possibly a drastic one, but it seemed to be the only course left
to her.

The vicarage was large, timbered and rambling. In the
spring and summer no doubt it looked very picturesque in its
setting of lawns, trees and flower-beds. Now, with decaying
leaves squelching underfoot and the bare branches writhing,
it was unbelievably dreary. The door was opened by Mrs.
Simpson, small and spry in powder blue.

"Oh! Mrs.—er—Bannerman, isn't it? Good afternoon."

"Good afternoon. I wonder if I could see the vicar for a
few minutes?"

"Yes, of course. Won't you come in?"

The hall was square, parquet-floored, and smelt of polish.

165

"He's working on his sermon, but I'm sure he'll be glad to see you." Mrs. Simpson tapped on a door. "Mrs. Bannerman would like a word with you, dear."

The vicar rose from behind his desk, his spectacles slipping forward over his nose. "Mrs. Bannerman! How nice! I do hope you're none the worse after the other evening."

Celia said steadily, "I'm afraid I'm very much the worse, Mr. Simpson." She caught the rather startled surprise in his wife's eyes and then the door closed behind her.

"Dear me, I'm sorry to hear that. Come and sit down." He pulled out a chair on one side of the desk. Behind him an old-fashioned radiator belched peevishly. Beyond the window the bare lawn stretched, dripping and deserted. "Now, how can I help you?"

"Mr. Simpson, may I ask you a rather curious question? Could you tell me, please, whether you believe in the devil?"

He stared at her for a moment, pushing his glasses back up his nose with one finger. "Well, that is rather a poser! Of course I know that Satan is referred to in the Bible but I fancy that nowadays we usually take that to mean a force of evil which, unfortunately, is only too obviously real."

"But why should we be prepared to personify the power of good and not that of evil?"

"Now that you ask me, I'm afraid I really couldn't say." He looked a little worried.

"Then you admit Satan might be real?"

"Indeed he might, my dear young lady. I certainly can't deny the possibility."

"Right, well now that we've established that, what would be your reaction if someone came to you and told you that it was now the devil's turn to be made man and he was at this very moment living here in Rychester?"

He stared at her, trying to gauge the seriousness of her

166

question. "I imagine," he said after a moment, "that I would be seriously alarmed, but I have to admit I'm not sure whether my alarm would not be chiefly for that person's state of mind."

"In other words, the devil too would find it hard to convince people who he really was. But then he probably wouldn't want them to know anyway."

Mr. Simpson cleared his throat. "Might I ask, Mrs. Bannerman, where these rather strange questions are leading?"

Celia looked down at her tightly laced hands. "Mr. Simpson, there is nothing at all wrong with my state of mind, I can assure you."

He leant forward incredulously. "You mean—? You're surely not trying to tell me that you—?"

"I'm trying to tell you that I am convinced that the devil *is* here, now, and things are going very much his way."

"You—aren't speaking metaphorically, by any chance?"

"I'm afraid not. I could take you to him now. I know it sounds—unbalanced. We're just not programmed to accept such things, but then neither were the Galileeans."

After a moment of intense scrutiny of her face, he sat back and folded his hands on the desk. "I think perhaps you'd better tell me everything from the beginning."

So once more she went through it, her voice dropping into the silent room which surely had never heard such words before. She told him of Lucas's hypnotic gaze, of the spellbinding power of his playing, of Lucy's phenomenal progress. She mentioned the child's alleged perception of auras and that she insisted Lucas had none. She told of Eva's wax dolls, the scrap of paper with the spell on it. She even recounted, with shuddering revulsion, how Lucas had seized her hand and sucked greedily at her finger. She went on to enumerate the disasters that had befallen them, culminating

167

now in Tom's illness. When at last she stopped speaking, it seemed that her disembodied words still blundered about the room like a host of ugly, menacing bats.

Mr. Simpson cleared his throat again. "Mrs. Bannerman, I need hardly tell you that this is not going to be easy. Have you mentioned your suspicions to anyone else?"

"Some of them, yes, to my brother and sister. They didn't believe me. I can hardly blame them. But you're trained to believe in the supernatural. You're my last hope."

"What is it that you want me to do?"

"Quite literally, to deliver us from evil. Perform an exorcism."

"I'm not qualified to do that personally, I'm afraid. I should have to seek advice from the appropriate quarter." He hesitated. "In any case, it may hardly be applicable, since you say this man is not *possessed* by the devil but is the devil himself." He glanced across at her intent face. "You know, I feel bound to suggest that whereas your own mind might be perfectly healthy, it is highly likely that this Mr.—ah—Todd's is not. From what you tell me it certainly sounds as if he is mentally ill. This is not to say that he mightn't be a real danger, to himself as well as to others. As you probably know, there is a type of madness that takes the form of being convinced one is someone famous—usually Napoleon or Hitler, I believe. Then there's your stepsister, who undoubtedly appears to have been dabbling in the black arts. That is enough in itself to turn her mind. We are warned very specifically in the Bible about the dangers of such practices."

"Then what do you suggest I should do?"

"Pray, my dear, for them as well as yourself. Pray hard and keep on praying."

"I tried," Celia said in a low voice, "but the words jumbled up meaninglessly in my head. I heard Lucy praying 'Deliver

168

us to evil' and after that I was afraid to try, in case I ended by damning myself."

"Will you try again now, with me?"

She shook her head miserably. "I daren't."

"Then kneel with me, while I pray for both of us."

The words he said were much more suitable to the room's atmosphere than those she had spoken, but they skittered across the surface of her mind and she was unable to retain them. She rose to her feet a little self-consciously.

Mr. Simpson took off his glasses and polished them vigorously. "We clergy are sometimes accused of being impractical," he commented with a slight twinkle. "In an attempt to disprove that, I'm perfectly willing to come with you to see this—ah—gentleman."

"Oh, would you? I should be so grateful."

"I'm not sure quite what would come of it, but no doubt it would help to crystalize my own thoughts on the matter and we could take it from there. I have the feeling that you think there is no time to lose, so would tomorrow afternoon be convenient?"

"It would have to be after school."

"He teaches in your husband's school?" The vicar's voice had sharpened.

"Yes. Think of the potential he has there." Celia picked up her bag and gloves. "Thank you so much for hearing me out."

He walked with her to the front door. She said suddenly, "Be careful, Mr. Simpson. If he knows I've approached you—"

"I shall be all right, don't worry. I'll call at your house, then, about four-thirty tomorrow."

"That will be fine. Thank you."

"Good afternoon, Mrs. Bannerman. God bless you."

169

"Amen," she murmured fervently.

As she hurried along St. Peter's Road the sky was already darkening and at the corner of Regent's Walk the rain began, heavy, deliberate drops merging quickly into one another on the pavement. She ran up the hill and into Cavendish Road while the deluge darkened the shoulders of her coat and dripped uncomfortably down her neck. At her own gate she glanced up at the bedroom window. The light was on. Either Tom had been up or Eva was already home.

CHAPTER 13

THE dream that night was the worst she had known. She was in the middle of a dark, menacing wood and the trees reached out for her as she passed, green malignant eyes glowing between the branches. She was lost and terrified but she didn't know what she was running from. Suddenly the trees seemed to leap apart, creating a clearing much the same as the one she had seen in her dream of Pan. But this time a hastily constructed altar had been set up, complete with flaring candles, squat and white like those in Eva's room. And hanging limply and apparently lifelessly over the altar lay Tom. She tried to run forward but her feet had literally taken root and she plunged full length to the ground, the sharp twigs and stones cutting her face. Despairingly she stretched out her arms toward the crumpled figure but he was beyond her reach. Then Lucas and Eva materialized on either side of the altar, Eva in long black robes like a medieval priestess, and both of them towering upwards so that their heads were among the branches of the tall trees.

"Save him, save him!" Celia was crying, but Eva had taken a sacrificial knife from her belt and was testing the blade against her thumb. And Lucas's voice spoke in her head, though his lips did not move. "Only you can save him."

She woke with pounding heart to find Tom moaning softly

171

beside her and she flung herself against him, holding his burning body close to her. For the hours that remained till morning she lay awake, terrified even to close her eyes lest the dream return. She had a superstitious dread that if in the dream Eva should use her black-handled knife, she would wake to find Tom lying dead beside her.

Friday the thirteenth of December. The day she had arranged for Mr. Simpson to come face to face with his legendary adversary. Her wild, disjointed thoughts tumbled over each other in confusion. She imagined herself leading Mr. Simpson into a room full of people and saying to him, "Whomsoever I shall kiss, that same is he." Her mind skidded away from the implied blasphemy and she tried in vain to remember the vicar's soothing words of prayer. But all that filled her head were the words Eva had spoken in that vibrating, reverent voice: "And to thee, oh Prince of Darkness, my soul pays eternal homage. *Probatum, probatum, probatum.*"

Stiff with fear, she tried to make her mind a complete blank since she had no control over the words that came flooding into it. How had she become so involved with these forces? She had not wanted to, had not tried to bargain with them despite the tempting prizes they had paraded before her. She had done nothing positive, but she had allowed herself to drift and that had been enough. She had acquiesced to Lucy's lessons against her better judgment, she had gone alone to Lucas's flat after Frances's death. With Eva's undermining influence in her own home, nothing more was needed.

Daylight seeped slowly into the room. Wearily she dragged herself out of bed and went down to make breakfast. At eleven o'clock Mr. Simpson phoned.

"Mrs. Bannerman, I'm so terribly sorry—I shan't be able

172

to meet you this afternoon. I slipped on some ice outside the front door and my ankle is badly sprained. But my curate would—"

"It doesn't matter," she said heavily. After all, she must not incapacitate the whole staff of St. Peter's.

"Indeed it does matter. Mr. Philips is a most devout and sincere man—"

"It's all right, Mr. Simpson. Really."

"But you so obviously need help."

"Yes."

"I shall of course continue to pray for you, but Mr.—"

"Thank you."

"If you change your mind, you have only to telephone. Mr. Philips could come this afternoon as arranged or, if there is no immediate urgency my ankle should be better in a few days."

"Thank you," she said again. He was only humouring her. For all his reassurance the day before, he probably did think she was mentally ill or neurotic in some way. He might even be right. Everyone else seemed to think so. Only Eva knew she told the truth and Eva was not likely to speak in her defense.

Slowly she walked back to the kitchen and stood staring out the window. A squirrel ran on the lawn, tail trailing, searching busily for his hidden store of nuts. It was almost time for Tom's medicine, though it seemed a shame to wake him. Alan had made his usual early morning call and seemed perturbed that the drugs were making no improvement in Tom's condition. He said he would call in again that evening. Eva's college broke up for Christmas today, although the school had another week to go.

Christmas. Its approach filled Celia with dread. She had made no preparations other than the puddings she had been making when Martin called a few weeks ago. Would it be safe to leave Tom with Eva next week while she did some prolonged shopping? The internal telephone on the wall buzzed suddenly, making her jump.

"Celia? Why was I not told of Tom's illness? I met Angela at the shops just now and she told me he's in bed. I thought on Sunday he was looking rather drawn. What's wrong?"

"I don't know, Mother. I'm sorry I didn't think to tell you. So much seems to have been happening. We went to the carol concert on Wednesday and he was taken ill when we got home. Alan thought it might be flu but he doesn't seem to be responding to treatment."

"May I come down and see him?"

"Of course. Actually, if you wouldn't mind staying within call for an hour or two, I really ought to go into town." But not to Rawdons. She had no wish to encounter the suspicious Mr. York.

"Certainly I can stay. It's my duty, after all. I'm only surprised you didn't think to contact me earlier."

Mrs. Bannerman's sharp manner changed, however, when she saw Celia. "Good gracious, child, you look far from well yourself. Whatever has been happening here this week?"

"I haven't been sleeping well." She couldn't confide the trouble with Kate, nor would Mrs. Bannerman believe a word against Lucas. "And Eva has been rather difficult," she added, truthfully if less than fully.

"That doesn't surprise me. If you remember, I thought from the start that you were making a mistake in inviting her into your home, but as you know I don't believe in interfering. I'll stay with Tom, certainly, but I don't think you're in any condition to go wandering off into town. The shops are very crowded at this time of the year."

The unexpected kindliness in the remark penetrated Celia's defensive sheath and the slow, weakening tears started again. "But Mother, it's less than two weeks till Christmas and I haven't done a thing! I haven't even bought any cards."

"That's not like you, Celia. You're usually so efficient and well organized. Never mind now, dry your eyes. I'm not in my dotage yet and I'm quite prepared to take over the Christmas preparations."

"But I can't expect you to—"

"Nonsense!" Edith Bannerman interrupted briskly. "It's very pleasant to feel needed, after all this time. We can go down together at the beginning of next week, when the shops are a little less busy, for you to choose your personal gifts, but you may leave all the catering arrangements to me. I shall enjoy seeing to them. Now, I'm going to fill this hot-water bottle for you. Take it up the girls' room and lie down for a while. I'll stay with Tom."

There was great relief in allowing someone else to take control. Meekly Celia did as she was told, though she was naggingly aware that Tom appeared more ill than his mother had been prepared to find him. She left them together and, clutching the hot-water bottle, crept into Kate's bed and closed her eyes. Within minutes the warmth and the darkened room had their effect. She fell into deep, blessedly dreamless sleep and it was after two when she awoke to find her mother in-law by the bed with a bowl of chicken soup.

"I've just made some for Tom and I'm sure you're in need of something too. I'm afraid, though, that I can't persuade him to take any. I must say, Celia, I don't like the look of him at all."

"I know. Alan doesn't, either. He's calling again this evening. He's already given him various tests, but they've proved negative and he doesn't seem any nearer finding out what's wrong."

"Well, drink this while it's hot. I presume you had a good sleep."

"Wonderful, thank you. I feel much better able to cope now."

"That's good, but there's no need for you to do too much. I'm here now and I certainly don't see why Eva shouldn't do her share as well."

Alan was far from reassuring that evening. "Celia, I'm going to call in a second opinion. We just don't seem to be getting anywhere. Brewster's an excellent man; perhaps he'll be able to put his finger on the cause of it all. I've arranged to bring him round tomorrow morning." He looked at her closely. "You haven't been indulging in any more flights of fancy, have you? You look a bit under the weather yourself."

"I'm not going to argue with you, Alan," she said tiredly, "but I haven't changed my mind. I still believe implicitly in what I told you."

"I'd rather like you to see a specialist too, but we'll set Tom back on his feet first. Now be a good girl and try those pills I prescribed for you. At least they'll help you to relax."

She could hardly tell him she dared not relax. Instead, she said, "Mrs. Bannerman was a tower of strength today. I was just about at the end of my tether when she arrived and took over completely, packing me off to bed while she sat with Tom."

"Good. And I gather Eva will be home for a while now too. See that she pulls her weight. None of that airy-fairy floating off on her own concerns. It seems to me you've had to put up with altogether too much for the last few weeks. It's no wonder you cracked up. If Tom was really fooling around with her, he needs his head examined. Perhaps that was the first symptom of his illness!"

176

Celia smiled as she was meant to. "She arouses his protective instinct."

"She's more likely to 'arouse' the flat of my hand," Alan said grimly. "Seriously, though, you mustn't let your imagination run away with you. It can be really dangerous if something like that is allowed to go unchecked. By the way, Robert's home. He sent his love. He was all set to come round with me but I indicated firmly that this was hardly the time for social calls. You'll be intrigued to know he's found himself a new girl friend! Wants her to come and stay for some of the vac."

"Good for Robert. Give him my love, too. I'll look forward to seeing him in a day or two. Alan—" she put a hand on his arm as he turned toward the door. "Tom is going to —be all right, isn't he?"

His eyes were grave. "I very much hope so, love. I'm counting on Brewster for advice."

Mrs. Bannerman readily agreed to Celia's suggestion that she should forsake her own flat for the time being in favour of their guest room and the next morning, while the two doctors were closeted with Tom, they sat together drinking coffee, their ears straining for the sound of the opening bedroom door. Eva, despite Mrs. Bannerman's efforts, had disappeared. No doubt she had gone down to clean for Lucas Todd.

But when the doctors finally emerged, it appeared that Mr. Brewster was as puzzled as Alan. He recommended a change of prescription, but Celia had the uncomfortable feeling that it was all rather hit-and-miss and that it had not been possible to make an accurate diagnosis.

"It's extremely important that he shouldn't become dehydrated, Mrs. Bannerman. He has a high fever and must have plenty of liquids. Apart from that, just keep him warm and as comfortable as possible. The fever is quite likely to break within the next twenty-four hours or so."

The two men left together and Celia didn't have the chance of a private word with Alan. She knew that had he any concrete news to impart, he would phone her as soon as he reached home. There was no phone call, nor had she expected one.

The damp rawness of earlier in the week had cooled and brightened to a cold sunny morning, and suddenly the limp leaves and bare branches regained something of their beauty. Lucy was out in the garden, gathering armsful of fallen leaves and hurling them into the air. Celia watched her with an aching heart. If only she were a normal, affectionate little girl, with no latent powers to excite the interest of unholy powers. Kate, who had carefully kept out of her mother's way since their confrontation at Rawdons on Thursday, was still pale and sulky.

"Why did you do it, Kate?" Celia asked sadly, when at last she found herself alone with the child.

Kate eyed her defiantly. "It was your fault. Yours and Daddy's. I *told* you I needed more pocket money and you wouldn't give me any."

"That was no reason to resort to stealing."

"It wasn't stealing. At least, not for myself, so it doesn't count. All I took were Christmas presents, for you and Daddy and Grandma."

"Oh Kate!" Celia pulled the stiff little body into her arms. "Darling, you know we'd a hundred times rather have something small that you could afford or had made yourself."

"The girls at school said it was soppy to make bathsalts and things. They were *buying* presents for their families. I didn't see why I couldn't get proper things for you."

178

"Then you should have saved up your pocket money throughout the year. Daddy and I are always telling you not to spend it the minute you get it. If you put it away safely in the Post Office it would be there when you wanted it, and even a little bit extra as interest. But make no mistake about it, Kate, whatever your motives were, taking things that weren't paid for was definitely stealing."

Kate wriggled out of her arms and adroitly changed the subject. "How long is Daddy going to be in bed?"

"I don't know, dear."

"He's missing all the fun at school. We had the Fifth Form pantomime today and it was very funny. Clare Davis was King Rat, and do you know, with all the makeup and everything she looked just like Mr. Todd!" She giggled, looking up at her mother's frozen face. Lucas Todd was the last person of whom Celia wished to be reminded.

Eva appeared for lunch, as usual without volunteering any information of her whereabouts during the morning. Celia sensed a tightly controlled excitement in her, and her heart sank. Had she discovered the removal of Tom's clothes from her suitcase and the missing spell?

Celia had steamed some fish for Tom and dressed it in an appetizing sauce, but he only managed one mouthful before pushing the plate away. At least she was relieved that he was swallowing the jugful of blackcurrant and orange juice which she kept replenishing on his bedside table. In fact, he seemed to have an unquenchable thirst. The first dose of Mr. Brewster's prescription was duly taken, and Celia hoped fervently that this would mark the beginning of an improvement. She drew the curtains across the windows to shut out the hard bright sunlight and he obediently settled down to sleep.

Mrs. Bannerman was alone in the study reading the paper

when Celia went down. She dropped into a chair and closed her eyes but the restful quality she had loved about the room could not reach her. It was no longer timeless and unchanging. The clock on the mantlepiece ticked relentlessly and it was only too easy to imagine that it was ticking Tom's life away. She shied away from the thought, but the room had let her down in more ways than one these last weeks. She could still see Tom and Eva entwined on the sofa, hear Tom's broken words as, whisky bottle in hand, he told her of Ruth and the drugs. And Lucy's distorted prayer still hung on the air.

"Mummy!" Kate came running into the room, plaits flying and eyes wide with horror. "Mummy, come quickly! Lucy's caught a squirrel and she's—she's torturing it!"

It was indicative of her state of mind that while horror flooded through her, she felt no surprise. She flew after Kate out of the front door and round the side of the house to the garden shed, shivering in a mixture of cold and apprehension as the keen wind whistled through the material of her dress. Lucy met them at the door, her eyes hard and bright.

"Sneak!" she spat at her sister. "Tell-tale!"

Celia pushed her aside, acclimatizing her eyes to the dimness of the shed. On a shelf at the far end, in a dilapidated old bird cage, cowered a small grey form. "What were you doing to it?" Celia hardly recognized her own voice.

"It's only an animal, I don't know what all the fuss is! Squirrels are vermin, Daddy said so. It needs to be killed."

Celia turned to gaze unbelievingly at this stranger in her daughter's form: Lucy, who had always had a deep and passionate love for all living things—"Even ladybirds have coloured lights, Mummy"—who had sobbed at the death of a fly in a spider's web. Dazed, she moved nearer the cage to

180

encounter the terrified eyes behind the bars. "What were you doing to it?" she repeated stonily.

"I hadn't started properly."

"She was going to cut it up!" Kate burst out, and began to cry. Celia felt the vomit well up in a bitter flood and choked it down.

"Have you touched it at all? Hurt it in any way?"

"I didn't have time," Lucy said furiously. "Kate spoiled everything."

Murmuring broken little words of comfort to the petrified animal, Celia carefully carried the cage outside, set it down on the grass and opened the door. For a moment the creature could not believe escape was within reach. Then, suddenly, it moved. It wriggled through the small opening—how had Lucy manoeuvred it into the cage?—and fled blindly over the grass and up the side of the fence. Celia stood staring after it. There was nothing she could say to Lucy, nothing at all. If she so much as looked at that closed, cruel little face she felt her control would snap and she would lash out at her.

Without turning back to the shed, she walked woodenly round the house to the back door. She was still sitting in the kitchen, frozen into a hard shell of terror, disgust and despair, when the door opened and Martin came in.

"No one knew where you were, so I tried the usual place! How's Uncle?"

"Very ill." Her voice cracked. The boy moved swiftly over to her.

"What is it? What's happened?"

"Actually—" She moistened her lips. "I wasn't thinking of Tom just then. Martin, Lucy was—was trying to mutilate a squirrel. *Lucy!*"

He put his hand over her cold one. "Can you tell me about it?"

181

Stumblingly she recounted what had happened. "It's just one more thing," she finished dully, "one more horrible, beastly example of the depth to which we've all sunk."

"Celia, I know what you told Mother the other day. I heard her telling Dad—about Eva and Mr. Todd. They're worried about you. They think you're ill."

She nodded without speaking. He leant forward. "I'm worried, too. But in my case it's because I *don't* think you're imagining it." Her eyes swivelled to his face, young and earnest, trying to reassure her. "Celia, I had to come and tell you. I think you're *right*!"

Almost imperceptibly the coldness inside her began to melt. "You mean it? You believe what I said about Eva and Lucas?"

"Yes, I do. I can't see any other explanation for all that's happened."

"Oh Martin, the relief to hear you say that!" Her voice quivered. "At times I thought I was going mad. It seemed so fantastic, so appallingly impossible."

"I know a bit about it, you see," he offered modestly. "I read up quite a few books about mystics and gnosticism and so on. And after that discussion we had on Uncle's birthday, I also checked up on the latest experiments in telepathy. Remember what Uncle Alan said, about autosuggestion not necessarily being the reason for spells and death-wishes having effect? That it's possible for emotions and illness to be directed at someone, provided the sender can produce the right rhythm of brain waves?"

Celia stared at him. "You think—? Do you mean—?" She broke off and tried again. "Are you trying to say that's what's wrong with Tom?"

"Doesn't it fit? No one knows what this mysterious illness

182

is, but it came on pretty quickly and I gather that his deterioration has been fairly rapid. If you ask me, we've no further to look than Eva and Mr. Todd."

"The dolls!" Celia's voice was hardly audible. "I can't think why it didn't occur to me before! I suppose that at a basic level I just couldn't bring myself to believe it was possible. But *why*, Martin? What could they possibly have against Tom?"

"Search me. Look, it's quite likely I don't know the whole story. Mother could easily have forgotten something important. Tell me everything you can remember, right from the beginning. When did you first feel there was something strange about Lucas Todd?"

Stumblingly, prompted occasionally by Martin, she went through it all yet again, starting on that September morning when she awoke to a feeling of imminent danger. The only part she omitted, mainly from embarrassment, was Lucas's obsession with the little swellings on her finger and Lucy's. She ended with Eva's command, as she had knelt over Tom's collapsed body on Wednesday night, to go straight to Lucas.

"That seems to be it, then." Martin's voice rang with excitement. "For some reason or other, it's you they want. Perhaps they think they can get at you through Uncle? Do you think Uncle Alan could help? He seemed to know quite a bit about it."

"I'm afraid not. I went to him on Monday, before Tom was really ill, and he obviously thought I'd taken leave of my senses."

"But he admitted—"

"In theory, yes. Not, apparently, on his own doorstep."

"But it was he who was so explicit about the effectiveness of what Aunt Melanie referred to as mumbo jumbo."

183

"Again, in theory only. It's no good, Martin. I did my best to convince him. If I go to him now and say Tom has a spell on him, he's quite likely to have me put away somewhere for my own protection." She hesitated. "I tried Mr. Simpson too."

"The vicar?"

"Yes. I thought perhaps exorcism might work."

"Good grief! What did he say?"

Briefly she told him of their conversation and his subsequent telephone call. He was silent for a while, turning it all over in his mind. "If, incredible as it seems, Uncle's illness really does stem from—from sticking pins into a wax doll, apparently all we have to do is find this doll and destroy it."

"That's what I thought at first, but I'm afraid it's not as easy as that. Anything that is done to the doll happens to the person it represents."

She watched the dawning horror on his face. "And I thought I had the answer to everything! Then how *do* we get the spell removed?"

Celia said expressionlessly, "By my doing whatever it is they want."

"No!" His hand closed tightly over hers. "Think what you're saying!"

"But surely there's no choice. Either Tom dies or I go to them."

Outside the windows the short bright day was dying. Somewhere up in the dark trees the released squirrel would be settling down for the night. She could hardly see the boy's face across the table but neither of them made a move to put the light on. Somehow their conversation was more suitable to the semidarkness.

"Tell me what to do, Martin." It didn't occur to either

184

of them how the tables had turned.

"I think the best thing would be to tackle Eva. Tell her you know she's causing Tom's illness and ask her outright the price of removing the spell. At least we'll then know exactly where we stand. Once we know what we're faced with, we can plan the best way to go about it."

"It's not only Tom, of course," Celia said after a minute. "They've certainly got a hold on Lucy. She's equally ill, though in her mind—her soul rather than her body."

"Lucy's a child. She's probably already been persuaded to join them."

"Then I shall have to buy her out as well. It looks as though I shall have to go to him, Martin. Their lives are worth more to me than mine."

Martin said in a low voice, "Don't forget it would be your *everlasting* life you'd be forfeiting. I just don't see how I can stand by and let you do it."

"Well, at least I'll speak to Eva. As you said, we can decide on the next course of action when we've heard what she has to say." She smiled a little. "It's selfish of me, but I'm awfully glad you're not at Oxford at the moment, or I would have been completely alone."

"Perhaps it was supposed to work out this way. Anyway, I fully intend to take up my place next year, if they keep it open for me."

"Oh Martin, I'm so glad!"

"And I don't mind telling you that all this business has had quite a lot to do with making up my mind. Obviously we need all the help we can muster on our side. You'll speak to her tonight then?"

"Eva?" Her smile faded and she shivered. "Yes, I'll have to. We might not have much time."

"Phone me tomorrow and we'll arrange to meet some-where. Not here; after you've confronted her it won't be safe to talk in this house." He stood up. "I'll slip out the back door. I couldn't make polite conversation with Mrs. Bannerman now to save my life. Goodbye, Celia. And good luck."

CHAPTER 14

AFTER Martin had gone, Celia slowly rose from the table and moved toward the hall door, blinking in the light beyond it. As though recovering from a long illness, she made her way almost painfully up the hall. The sound of the television reached her from the study. She pushed open the door and glanced inside. Eva was curled up in her usual place with a book and the children, the nightmare of the afternoon incredibly forgotten, were side by side on the sofa, laughing at the Bruce Forsyth program. Unnoticed, Celia closed the door softly and went on up the stairs. The landing was lit only from the hall below except for a subdued glow from the half-open door of her own bedroom. Through the crack she could see Mrs. Bannerman sitting crocheting beside the bed. Stealthily, like a thief in her own house, Celia went up the flight of steps to Eva's room. This time there was no lingering guilt in her. It was imperative that she should find what she was looking for.

She did not waste time on the drawers or cupboards. Thursday's search, when Tom was already ill, would have revealed the doll had it been there. Nor, she knew, was it in the suitcase where his clothes had been. She stood for a moment in the middle of the room, her eyes moving systematically over walls and ceiling searching for a possible hiding place.

Firstly she carried a chair over to the window and reached up to run her fingers along the pelmet. Only dust was hidden there. She climbed up again to feel along the top of the wardrobe beside the case and discovered a forgotten tennis racket. Nothing else. Her eyes moved over the boarded up fireplace and then, abruptly, returned to it. She went quickly across and began to press and prize at the hardboard which covered the empty grate. With a suddenly dry mouth, she felt the screen move and give way under pressure. Carefully she laid it on one side and surveyed the black gaping hole of the fireplace. Trembling now, she pushed up her sleeve and reached up into the damp sooty darkness of the chimney. Almost immediately her searching fingers closed on a small, hard object, lodged precariously on a shelf of protruding brick. Carefully she withdrew it and stood gazing down at the worn-away image of her husband. The doll had changed greatly from when she had last seen it, smiling in its box alongside the others. This was one of the wax figures and at last Celia knew at least one of the uses of the candles. Regularly day by day the small figure must have been held in a flame until its wax began to melt and the doll to shrivel. Quite literally, Tom's image was wasting away. As was Tom himself.

A breath of air rather than a sound spun her round and Eva stood just inside the door. "I knew you'd find it when you were desperate enough," she said calmly.

Celia's bare arm was cold and smudged with soot. She clutched the doll convulsively as though she feared Eva might try to wrest it away from her. "Why?" she asked numbly. "Why are you doing this to him?"

"It seemed to be necessary, to force you to go to the

Master. You've known for some time that he wants you but you've been stupid and stubborn and refused to go to him. We thought perhaps it was loyalty to Tom that was holding you back, that if you thought he was playing around you might give in. However, you didn't, so it seemed he would have to be removed more permanently."

"But *why* does he want me so much?" Celia whispered.

"You really don't know, do you?" Eva came slowly toward her, her huge dark eyes as empty-looking as holes in a turnip head at Hallowe'en. "He wants you, my dear Celia, because, for all your moral indignation and high-faluting ideas, there is no denying one basic, gloriously ironic fact. *You're a witch yourself!*"

The white disc of the girl's face, slashed with the black line of hair, tilted and began to spin slowly. Eva caught hold of her to prevent her from slipping to the ground in blessedly unconscious oblivion.

"Listen to me, Celia! I'm a converted witch, yes, but you're fortunate enough to be a hereditary one, and so of course is Lucy. All the power she has comes from you."

Her head felt overlarge and heavy, a turnip in its turn. Were her eyes as vacantly staring as Eva's? She moved her thick tongue and said at last, indistinctly, "It's—not true." But there was no hope in her to support her disclaimer.

Eva seized her soot-grimed hand and raised it triumphantly. "The wart! Now do you believe me? All true witches have warts, you must know that. They're symbolic teats—to suckle the devil." The wave of revulsion shook Celia with such violence that she felt her body must fall apart. She could only stand helplessly with burning eyelids shut tightly against the obscene memory which tormented her, but there was no way of closing her ears to Eva's quiet, gloating voice.

"I admit I didn't realize what you were," she went on, "though I knew, of course, about Lucy. She's a very gifted child with strong natural powers. As I told you, I called up the Master for help in training her. But the first time he saw you he recognized your own powers and was determined to win you over. He has been very patient with you. I asked him once why he didn't simply enforce your allegiance, as he was perfectly capable of doing. He said, 'I could, of course, but I would prefer that she came of her own accord. Then there is no going back.' "

There was a pause and Celia forced her eyes open as her brain searched frantically for some escape from the monstrous charges laid against her. "It can't be true," she stammered shakily at last. "A great many people have warts. Are you telling me they're all witches?"

"Of course not. But yours will glow purple if I say the necessary words, as Lucy's does. She recognized the Master subconsciously from the start. Remember, the first time he came, how she called him Lucifer?" She smiled. "And by the way, witches are unable to repeat the Lord's Prayer." But Lucy had managed it eventually. Perhaps there was still a glimmer of hope. "So if you really want to save Tom— though personally I don't think he's worth saving: After all, he's already sold his soul—all you have to do is go to the Master now, tonight."

Celia moistened paper-dry lips. "And if I go, what will I have to do?"

The girl's eyes glowed. "Acknowledge your heritage. Become initiated as a full witch."

"Then Tom will live?"

"If that's what you still want."

"There will be other conditions."

"Great Lucifer, you speak of conditions! You should be

190

everlastingly grateful for all the time and trouble that has been taken over you!"

"Even so, unless they're met I won't agree."

Eva was breathing quickly, her face twisted with sudden fury. "You fool! You're in no position to make bargains! Don't you realize you haven't a hope of withstanding him now?"

Tenaciously Celia clung to the only shred of comfort left to her. "If he wants me to go voluntarily, he must agree to my terms."

"Very well. Go to Front Street. If you dare, state your terms. I will have to abide by whatever the Master says, though I've felt all along he was far too gentle with you. He must consider you have strong latent powers and are worth the trouble."

The thought of the drive through the dark town and the man who would be awaiting her made Celia quail. She said faintly, "Couldn't you pass on the conditions if I tell you what they are?"

Eva gave a short laugh. "I wouldn't dare! For once in your life you can be humble. Go and beg for your miserable terms."

"What—what would be involved in initiation?"

"It's a full rite. There will be an altar with symbols laid on it—the sacred knife, the cauldron, the wand and the pentacle. There's a cord to signify unity and a scourge as a symbol of purity. And there is incense and candles. It's very awe-inspiring."

"But—this wouldn't take place tonight?"

"Of course not. It needs careful preparation. Usually a new witch serves a probationary period and must answer searching questions on the craft before she can attain full witchhood, but of course it is within the Master's jurisdiction to waive that and he has indicated that he will in your case. He intends to have you a full witch at the earliest moment possible. Probably the ceremony will be arranged for next weekend, the time of the winter solstice. It's our first sabbath of the year. Celia—" Eva took hold of her unwilling hand. "Let us be friends. You were good to me when I was a child and I have regretted the gulf which opened between us. I want you to know that I shall be happy to serve you in any way I can."

With an effort Celia extricated her hand. "I'll go to him, then."

"Yes." Gently Eva removed the doll from her clutching fingers. "Leave this with me. I have a feeling we won't be needing it again, but I must await confirmation."

Celia moved past her out of the room. She went first to the bathroom. The sticky, clinging soot was difficult to remove from her hand and arm and she rubbed at it furiously as though its removal would be a spiritual cleansing.

"Celia, is that you?" Mrs. Bannerman had come out onto the landing.

"Yes, Mother."

"I'm desperately worried about Tom. He—he almost seems to be sinking before my eyes." The old voice shook perilously. Celia bent and kissed her.

"It's all right, Mother. He'll start to get better very soon now."

Mrs. Bannerman stared at her, hope struggling with incredulity. "You think so? But how can you possibly know, when even the doctors are at a loss?"

"Just believe me. By this time tomorrow he will be sitting up asking for food."

"If only I could believe that!"

"I have to go out now. I expect only to be about an hour.

192

Then you must get some rest and I'll sit with him. Try not to worry."

It seemed to Celia that, with or without Lucy, she had been driving to Front Street since the beginning of time. As she drew up outside the flat she could see the figure of Lucas Todd outlined against the lighted first-floor window. As always the door was on the latch.

He was standing in the middle of the sitting-room waiting for her and she was immediately conscious of the change in him. This was no longer the suave and competent music master but a mighty prince imperiously awaiting her homage. Across the room she steadily met the impact of his gaze.

"Well?"

"You know why I'm here."

A ripple passed over his face. "It would be as well if you showed more deference in your manner. You no longer have the excuse of ignorance."

"I've come only because I have no option. I am prepared to bargain with you."

He said softly, "Once again I advise you to curb your tongue. You are fortunate to be admitted to this house at all after your actions the other day. Did you really imagine that mealy-mouthed old man would be a match for me?"

"But you didn't dare to risk meeting him, did you?"

His eyes blazed and immediately she regretted her foolhardiness. She braced herself, expecting physical violence, but with an effort he regained his self-control.

"You have spirit, Celia. The only reason I do not choose to crush it is that with the proper training it might prove useful to me. Nevertheless I shall not warn you again. Do you understand?"

After a moment she nodded.

"Very well. Then perhaps we may proceed to the object of

your visit. I presume you intend to weigh yourself against your husband's life?"

"In part, yes."

"In part?"

"Lucy must also be released."

His face congested with sudden fury. "You go too far! Lucy has received my personal tuition for the last three months. She has developed magnificently."

"If you had been content with her you would not have gone to such lengths to get me," Celia said.

"You imagine you are worth the lives of both your husband and daughter?"

"On the contrary. My own life is of no use to me without them. Unless you agree to release them, I shall kill myself and you will have gained nothing."

She saw the conflict in his face. "You mean that?"

"I do."

"Sit down, Celia." He motioned her to the sofa. "Let me explain why, as you put it, I went to such lengths to obtain you." He sat down opposite her, his face in the shadows but lit grotesquely from time to time by the leaping flames.

"I welcome a challenge, you see. Admittedly the worship of my followers is very agreeable and I would not be without it. But now and again, perhaps only once in several centuries, I find one who is unaware of her powers, who for some reason or another has no knowledge of the incredible forces within her. Then the element of the hunt enters into it. I stalk and I follow, allowing her brief glimpses from time to time of all she might achieve if she will only acknowledge her destiny. And I find more joy in that one—" his lips twisted into a mockery of a smile—"that one white sheep which I personally have nurtured than in all the black sheep who did

194

not have to be won over. You, Celia, could become such a one."

She thought: This has to be another dream. I cannot really be sitting in this pleasant flat here in Rychester talking to a man who believes himself to be Satan. But even if it were a dream, it must be played out to the end. She heard herself say, "Eva told me I'm a witch. Why should I believe her?"

He smiled slightly. "It would be more accurate to say you are a potential witch. You have all the powers required but they are dormant because you have never exercised them. If they are left untapped for very much longer they will fade altogether."

"So if I had never met you, I should have gone on being an ordinary normal person living an ordinary normal life?"

"Undoubtedly."

"And if I refuse now, once and for all, to be initiated, I should continue to be such a person?"

"Indeed. Except that you would be a widow whose daughter was a witch."

She trembled. "So I have no choice." She lifted her head, staring across at his red-shadowed face. "Very well. Tell me what I must do."

"You must take part in the full ritual of initiation. You will be issued with all the tools of the craft and instructed in the ways of increasing your powers. And once the initiation is performed, your husband's health will be restored."

"No," she interrupted. "That's not enough. He must be cured now. Eva said it will take some days to arrange the ceremony. Tom might not live that long."

"You drive a hard bargain," he said evenly. "Very well. If you insist the spell will be withdrawn tonight. But under-

195

stand that if you deviate in any way from your undertaking, it will swiftly be reimposed."

"Another thing. Tom offered his soul for a music master."

"I am aware of that."

"It was only a figure of speech. He didn't mean it."

"Then he should not have said it."

"His recovery won't be complete without his soul."

His mouth tightened. "Very well," he said again.

"And—Lucy?"

His hand struck the arm of his chair. "Is it not enough that I agree to save your worthless husband? Will you rob me of Lucy too? Think how pleasant it would be for you to have such an able assistant in your own home. You would work admirably together, you and Lucy."

"Unless you release her, the deal is off."

"But she has always had intuitive powers. I did not bestow them on her."

"She never used them for evil purposes before. If you withdraw the knowledge you have given her, she will be as she was."

"She may not thank you for this."

"She will know nothing about it. You must arrange that she forgets all the undercurrents of the last four months. From tonight."

"By Hecate," he said softly, "it is many years since I have paid so high a price."

"But you agree?"

"If I do not release Lucy, you will kill yourself?"

"Yes."

"Then since I could not permit such waste I agree." He leant forward suddenly. "Now, enough of such matters. I want to tell you of the wealth of secret knowledge you will acquire—clairvoyance, the properties of herbs, astral flight,

196

numerology—Oh Celia, there are so many exciting things to teach you! I fancy you will be an apt pupil. That is why I am prepared to postpone the learning time until after the initiation."

She said with an effort, "Is the spell ended now?"

"Yes, I have already instructed Eva." He saw her look of doubt, and added, "Telepathically, of course. And when Lucy wakes tomorrow she will be as she was at the end of August. You realize, of course, that to repay my generosity a great deal will be expected of you?" She nodded dumbly. "Do not look so apprehensive!" he chided her gently. "Your life will not change outwardly unless you wish it. It will merely become richer from within. All that you desire you will achieve, but your prattling sister, your well-meaning brother and your more than fortunate husband will not notice any difference in you."

Celia wrenched her eyes away from his glowing, hypnotic gaze. "I must go. I told Mrs. Bannerman I wouldn't be long."

"I should prefer you to stay and begin to understand some of the treasures in store for you, but if your mind is on other things it would be of no value. I will curb my impatience, now that I know the time of waiting is nearly over."

His eyes flickered to her hand and instinctively she covered the tell-tale finger. "So be it," he said softly. "We have eternity before us." He stood up and she stumbled to her feet. "I shall not see you again until the ceremony. It is better that way. And I trust," he added mockingly, "that the medical profession will be astounded at the sudden and inexplicable improvement in your husband. Good-night, Celia. I shall send you rewarding dreams."

As she reached the waiting car, the light in the window above went out. She crept inside and laid her burning forehead against the steering wheel. What in heaven's name could she do now to escape her commitment? In a trance she switched on the ignition and drove slowly home.

Mrs. Bannerman met her in the doorway. "Celia! My dear, I really believe you were right! Tom's skin is much cooler and he's breathing normally, instead of that horrible, shallow rasping. However could you have known it would happen?"

In the shadows behind her, Eva moved softly up the stairs.

"I just—hoped," Celia said faintly. Thank you, she thought fervently, and it was not Lucas Todd she was addressing. Thank you for saving Tom and Lucy. And now— please help me to save myself.

CHAPTER **15**

BY the next morning the improvement in Tom was noticeable enough for everyone to exclaim over. Lucy's recovery was not so apparent, since only Celia had been aware of the extent of her degeneration. She had a slightly puzzled air but there was nothing left of the calculating cruelty of the child who only the day before had with difficulty been restrained from torturing a squirrel. And the wart on her finger had disappeared overnight.

Martin phoned mid-morning. "Celia, what happened? Did it work?"

"Yes. Tom and Lucy are safe."

"Thank God."

"Yes," she agreed numbly.

"All right if I call for you after lunch? We'll go for a drive."

"I'll be ready."

"Now," he instructed a few hours later, as she pulled the car door shut behind her, "tell me everything that happened."

Tonelessly she related the finding of the wax doll in Eva's chimney and the subsequent visit to Lucas, but her voice sharpened as the car crossed the High Street and turned down Smugglers' Walk. "Where are we going?"

"I thought a walk along the prom might clear our heads."

"As long as we don't go anywhere near 56 Front Street!"

"No, I'll turn off along Water Lane and drive right down to the end. That's a good couple of miles from His Lordship."

They parked the car at the far end of the promenade and started to walk slowly, their bodies bent against the strong wind. "So he actually admitted who he was?"

"Not in so many words but it was certainly implied."

"It's unbelievable, isn't it? Have you any idea when they hope to hold this ceremony?"

"Eva said probably next weekend. It's the winter solstice or something."

"As soon as that? It doesn't leave us much time."

"I don't see what we can do anyway. He has the upper hand; if I don't go, he'll simply reclaim Tom and Lucy." She drew a deep shuddering breath. "Believe me, Martin, I've been over and over it looking for a way out but there just isn't one. I've accepted it now. If there's no help for it, I'm prepared to go through with it."

"Well, I'm not prepared to let you," he answered grimly. "We'll have to think of something. I'm afraid the conventional methods of resisting the devil aren't much help when you literally come face to face with him. Isn't there some theory about driving a wooden stake through his heart?"

Celia smiled a little. "I believe that only works with vampires. If I do go through with it, though, need anything very terrible happen? I mean they can't *force* me to do wrong, surely? I could be initiated and then just—let the matter rest. If I can convince them that I'm willing enough but not as powerful as they thought, perhaps they'll lose interest."

"No, Celia, it's out of the question. In any case, the initiation itself is an ordeal you can't possibly go through."

200

"It didn't sound too terrible. Lucas was telling me about it."

Martin glanced at her and then away again. "Did he mention *hieros garnos*?"

"I don't think so. What's that?"

"The—'sacred marriage.' I'm afraid these initiation rites are pretty basic."

Celia stopped dead, staring at him, and as his meaning became clear colour flooded her face. "Oh no," she said quickly, "I'm sure you're wrong there. Lucas isn't—interested in anything like that."

"Normally he may not be, but he won't be normal on this occasion. He'll have worked himself up to the right pitch of excitement with candles and incense and slow, throbbing music and probably hallucinatory drugs as well. Make no mistake about it, Celia, he will expect to make you the Devil's Bride."

She said in a strangled voice, "What can we do?"

"Our only hope seems to be to fight them with their own weapons. Unfortunately there are no textbooks on Satan, but there are on witches and one thing they believe in implicitly is the strength of will-power. They hoist 'cones of power' to deal with emergencies. Apparently this involves using their life force and often kills some of them, which is why it's kept as a last resort."

"Go on," she said drily.

"Well, I was just thinking that if we could muster enough people to direct their wills against Eva and Lucas—who wouldn't be expecting any opposition anyway—"

"It's hopeless, Martin. For one thing we can't even get the family to see the danger, let alone the hundreds we'd need to do any good. And for another, this immense control of will must be something which has to be worked at for years to

201

have any effect. And we have six days at the most."

They walked in silence past the shuttered ice cream booths and amusement arcades. It all seemed unreal to Celia. With the gnawing anxiety of Tom's illness suddenly removed, anticlimax had closed over her and she couldn't struggle free of it to a sense of her own peril. There was rain in the wind now and they turned and made their way back to the car.

"I've been pretty useless, haven't I?" Martin said in a low voice. "I was your only means of help and I've failed you. I simply don't know what to do."

"Perhaps if you went to Mr. Simpson—?" Celia suggested.

"I don't know that he'd be much help. The church, yes, but someone who has a wider knowledge of these things." He looked up suddenly, excitement on his face. "I know who *might* help us! There was an incredible chap—a bishop, I think—who came and lectured us once on the supernatural. It was a strictly 'thou shalt not' affair but he did admit, under questioning afterwards, that he had performed exorcisms. I'll have his name among my notes. Now, if I could persuade him of the urgency—"

"We can always hope," Celia said. She didn't want to dampen the boy's excitement but suppose this bishop was abroad, on missionary work, say, among the witch doctors, or had moved and no one had his address, or had died—?

"I'll drop you off at home and go straight back to look through my papers. It would probably be best if I don't contact you—we can't talk on the phone anyway and if I start calling daily Eva might get suspicious. But you can rest assured I'll do everything possible now to track down this man and in the meantime if there's any change of plan let me know at once. I doubt if there will be, though. They're great on ritual, these people, and if Sunday is one of their sabbaths

202

they'll probably wait till then. Cheer up, Celia, we're not beaten yet!"

During the following week an atmosphere of relief and gaiety filled the house. Tom continued to make excellent progress and Mr. Brewster's change of prescription was given far more credit than was its due. Lucy was brighter and happier than she had been for some time and even Kate seemed to be reverting to her old self. Only Celia appreciated that Eva's obvious happiness was based on other prospects than theirs.

As promised, Mrs. Bannerman went with Celia to the High Street and they embarked together on a bout of Christmas shopping. Brightly lit trees glowed in every shop window, counters were heaped with sparkling baubles. With surprising ease Celia selected all her purchases, each just right for the intended recipient. She chose, wrote and despatched Christmas cards while Mrs. Bannerman, flushed and triumphant, reigned in the kitchen over growing supplies of mince pies, stuffings and sauces. And through it all Celia moved in a dream, waiting, marking time. By Christmas, only such a short time away, what would have happened to her?

And then, earlier than she had expected, the summons came. One dark afternoon as she threaded the latest Christmas cards on the chain round the study wall, Eva approached and laid a hand on her shoulder. She turned swiftly, instant coldness claiming her. The girl's face was white with excitement, her eyes abnormally bright. "Tonight," she said softly. "It's been arranged for tonight."

"But—I thought it was to be Sunday?"

"All is ready. There is no point in delay."

Celia's mouth was dry. "What must I do?"

"I'm going down now to put the last touches to everything. There is nothing for you to do. Just come. You will be told your part in detail then. *Motte a ye.*" She turned and was gone, leaving the strange salutation unexplained in the suddenly apprehensive room. Its foreignness recalled those other words that Martin had spoken. *Hieros garnos.* Fear, unleashed at last, welled up in her. She fled to the telephone.

"Martin, dear?" Angie's voice was infuriatingly calm and unhurried. "I'm afraid he's not here. He went up to London for a few days, quite out of the blue. Said there was someone he had to see, or something. Naturally he didn't bother to explain."

An intolerable weight settled over her. "You don't know when he'll be back?"

"Not really. He said something vague about the end of the week. It could be tomorrow, or even later this evening."

"Will you tell him—" Celia's mind raced—"tell him I have to see him urgently. That the—the performance has been brought forward to tonight."

"The performance? How mysterious! What are you two hatching?" Angie laughed lightly. "Very well, I'll tell him. How's Tom?"

"Very much better, thank you." But she couldn't stop to think of Tom now. He was safe, as was Lucy. It was she herself who was in mortal peril with no one at hand who could save her.

Tom came slowly along the hall. "Mother's just put the kettle on, darling."

She said woodenly, "I have to go out."

"What have you forgotten now? Never mind, it can wait till after tea, surely."

She forced a smile and studied his face, already beginning to fill out again, less and less resembling that macabre wax

204

image. A fit of trembling seized her. She had to go. There was no choice. She couldn't risk his sliding further into the symbolic flame of Eva's candle. The full force of her love for him swept over her. He had been restored to her as his August self, before this fatal autumn term had refashioned him. The irritability, the brusqueness had all gone. Perhaps at last he had weathered the dire destiny that Eva's Tarot cards foretold.

"Hey, sweetheart, why the long face? This is the festive season!"

"Oh Tom!" She buried her face for a moment against his shoulder, feeling his arm come round her.

"What is it, love?"

"Nothing." Resolutely she straightened. "Just that I love you very much."

He kissed her gently. "That goes for me, too."

"Tea's ready!" Kate came skipping from the kitchen with a plate of mince pies. "Grandma said we could have these today, to celebrate breaking up. She's bringing the tray."

"Where are Eva and Lucy?" Mrs. Bannerman asked, going ahead of them into the study, and laying down the tray on the low table before the fire. With a dull pain Celia recognized her mental image of the room, safe and warm with its curtains drawn and the firelight glinting on the silver teapot. Would she ever be able to sit here again, surrounded by her family and with contentment in her heart? The room too had been freed by the terms of her bargain with Lucas, cleansed of the words and pictures which had smeared it for her. All was again as it should be—but at what a price.

Kate answered her grandmother. "I think I heard Eva go out, but Lucy's just coming."

Lucy slid into her place on the sofa, eyes shining with excitement. "I've wrapped up the last of my parcels now."

She looked at Celia and concern spread over her face. "Mummy, your light's all blue and wavery. What's the matter?"

"Mummy's just tired," Tom said quickly, "and no wonder, with all of us to look after. Leave her and her lights alone!" He smiled at Celia, humouring the child as they had always done.

"Surely you want a mince pie, Mummy?" Kate asked, holding out the plate despite Celia's shaken head.

"Not just now, darling."

"Saving up for supper!" nodded Lucy understandingly. Would she be back in time for supper? And would she really seem unchanged to them, as Lucas had promised, in spite of being made the Devil's Bride?

She laid down her cup and saucer quickly. "I'm afraid I must go out for a while," she said, marvelling at the steadiness of her voice. "I should be back in time for supper, but don't wait for me if I'm delayed." She stood up, her eyes going round their faces, rosy in the firelight, as though to imprint them forever on her memory; this one moment in time when they were together, complete—for the last time. Whatever Lucas said, she accepted that it would not be the real Celia Bannerman who returned later that night.

The bedroom was cold after the warmth downstairs, the bed rumpled from Tom's afternoon rest. Swiftly she straightened it. With icy hands she brushed her hair, put on fresh lipstick and went down again. She paused longingly at the telephone. Help me, Martin. Now. But it remained silent. She shrugged into her heavy coat and, like an exile, let herself out of the house. The light from the study window poured across the grass. It took all her strength to keep on walking. She did not take the car. She was incapable of driving it.

The park was closed, dark and silent behind its railings.

206

On the corner of Regent's Walk she passed a group of wool-en-hatted carol singers, swinging lanterns and laughing among themselves. The High Street shops, open late this Friday before Christmas, were still filled with people. She glanced wistfully in the windows. If only she could slip inside, mingle with the anonymous crowds. But destiny was waiting to claim her tonight. Inside her warm mitten the wart on her finger pulsed and throbbed.

Into Smugglers' Walk and down its narrow street past the temptingly displayed antiques, past the dark school building, closed from today for the Christmas holidays, and so on to Front Street and the sea breeze in her face. There was no light in the upstairs room of number fifty-six. She pushed the door open and went up the stairs. At the top Eva awaited her. She was dressed in a loose-fitting robe embroidered most exquisitely with strange patterns.

"This way," she said softly, leading Celia not to the sitting-room but along the corridor to a small bedroom. Laid out on the bed was a robe similar to Eva's.

"First, drink this." Eva handed her a beautiful silver chalice with symbols engraved on it—a cockerel, a bell, some crossbones.

"What is it?"

"An elixir. Just drink it."

Since there was no help for it, Celia raised it to her lips. Her mouth was still warm from the tea at home and the strange liquid struck cold and sweet. She drained the cup and handed it back.

"Now, will you please undress and put on the robe. Later it will be necessary to remove it. Clothes tend to bind the current through which the magic works. We find we are better without them. When you are ready, come to the room directly opposite. We will be waiting for you." She slipped out with a rustling of silk. With stiff, fumbling fingers Celia undid her coat. One by one she folded her clothes and laid them neatly on the bed. Though she shivered continuously with fear and apprehension, the room was actually very warm. She picked up the silken robe and slipped it over her head, its coldness softly caressing her warm body. Oh Martin, come now—before it's too late! How long dare she delay? They were waiting for her. On an impulse she dropped to her knees, the robe billowing about her. She bowed her head, but the only words she could form were: Help me! Help me! Perhaps they would be enough.

Stiff and sick she rose and moved to the door. The flat was silent, expectant. How many of these strange rituals had been celebrated here? She forced herself to cross the corridor and push open the door opposite, and immediately all contact with reality, with the sane world outside, fled.

The entire room, which was not large, was draped in black material of some kind which completely masked walls and window. All around it burned dozens and dozens of stout white candles and their tallow scented the air, vying with the cloying sweetness of incense. A large chalk circle had been drawn on the floor and in the center of it stood a black-draped altar on which were laid the tools of which Eva had spoken—a knife, a wand, a cauldron. But Celia's startled eyes, having swept the room, came fearfully back to the figures of Lucas and Eva standing on either side of the altar as they had in her dream; except that this time they were naked. Eva wore only a twisted metal band round her forehead and Lucas a strange, horned headdress. His eyes as they met hers were alight with an almost manic excitement and she remembered sinkingly what Martin had said about drugs.

208

"Welcome, sister," Eva said softly. "Come forward and make courtesy and due observance."

Slowly Celia moved into the room and briefly inclined her head. Eva would have insisted on a deeper obeisance but Lucas moved his hand slightly and she went on to the next stage of welcome. The potion which Celia had drunk must have clouded her brain and the girl's words did not penetrate it. She noticed for the first time the couch in the corner of the room, also shrouded in black, and its purpose shrieked silently in her head.

Levitation — mediumship — precognition — The words moved round the room like a swarm of brightly coloured flies. She felt herself sway and immediately Eva broke off her incantation. "Are you not well, sister?"

"It's—so hot."

Again Lucas made a small gesture and Eva moved to the side of the room, fumbled behind the drapery and pushed open the windows. Immediately the night wind rushed in, bending the flames of the candles and swirling along the floor over their bare feet. On and on went Eva's voice. It occurred to Celia that Eva was also in the grip of some strange drug, for her eyes were now becoming glazed and her voice had taken on a rhythmic, sing-song quality.

Celia's attention was drawn back to the candles, their light alternately leaping and crouching in the gusts of wind. Was it only in her imagination that they were bending ever nearer the black draperies on the wall, which, in their turn, seemed to billow out toward them? Fancifully Celia imagined them, candle and cloth, male and female, straining ever closer until they achieved the longed-for merging in the conflagration which would consume them.

Eva had progressed to a list of the deities. Some of the names were familiar—Diana the Moon Goddess, Hecate, by whom Lucas had sworn the other day. Other names were meaningless to her—Aradia, Faunus, Astarte. Her speech had slid now almost imperceptibly into a strange sixteenth-century English which made it increasingly difficult to understand. The draught Celia had swallowed had dulled her senses to the point where she felt completely detached from the pagan scene she was witnessing, a bystander incuriously watching the ceremony from a safe distance. And with increasing fascination her eyes were drawn again and again to the blowing cloth and the straining flames of the candles. All round the room now, cloth and flame bent closer and closer.

With wide, sweeping gestures of her arm, Eva scattered salt and water over the chalk circle and over the ritual instruments on the altar, calling as she did so on the ancient gods of north, south, east and west.

A slight sizzling sound behind her made Celia turn and as she watched, an orange tongue of flame licked out suddenly to the wind-inflated material and began to creep up it. And still the inhibiting liquor she had drunk dulled her senses to such effect that she was insensible of danger. She was vaguely aware that there was something she should do, aware also that her brain was not functioning at its normal speed. No doubt this passivity had been induced to make easier her coming ordeal with Lucas. Overlaying the scent of incense now the odour of smouldering cloth stung her nostrils. She said softly, "The draperies are on fire."

"Fire!" Eva repeated exultantly, "Fire symbolizes the life force as the cauldron does the womb of the Great Earth Mother. Now circle and instruments are purified. Come forward, sister, and make your vows."

There was a rending sound over on the far side of the room and a sheet of flame tore its way up the wall. A moment later the whole panel disintegrated and fell blazing onto the couch,

210

making it smoulder in its turn. The beginnings of fear at last stirred in Celia's sluggish brain. This could not after all be part of the ceremony.

"Eva—the fire is spreading!"

"We called on the god of fire and he has answered our call!" Eva declaimed.

Celia turned frantically to Lucas but he, like Eva, stood rock-still, his crazed eyes staring into space. "We must put out the fire!" she said more loudly, but even as she spoke she realized this was no longer possible. Separate tunnels of flame were now inching their way across the cloth masking the ceiling and even as she watched the curtains over the window went up in a roar of flame, fanned by the wind rushing in from the night outside.

"Eva!" Celia stumbled forward and caught the girl's bare arm, trying to drag her toward the door, but she slipped out of her hold. "Eva, wake up! We must get out while we can!"

Through the uncovered window now she could hear cries of alarm, running footsteps. With a frenzied lunge she again seized Eva, pulling her inch by inch across the floor. Wildly Eva began to laugh, throwing back her head, and to her numb horror Celia saw that her hair was on fire. She let go of her and started to beat at the flames with her hands but in the moment of release Eva ducked away and sped back to where Lucas still stood unmoving, apparently unscathed amid the sheets of flame. She flung herself down before him, clasping his legs, and above the crackle of the flames Celia heard her cry, "Take me with you, Master!"

With a thundering roar the burning drapery across the ceiling fell to the ground, igniting everything it landed on and bringing down some plaster with it. The heat was intense and Celia's burned hands throbbed painfully. It was now impossible to reach the others. With a conscious effort she tore

211

herself away from the awesome sight of the two figures locked together among the flames. Sobbing and stumbling with terror, she half fell down the staircase, colliding as she opened the door with the first of a crowd of men who were running up the path with hose-pipes and buckets of water.

"Hurry, there are two people inside!" she told them, pressing herself to the side to allow them to pass. Then she ran out along the road, adroitly dodging the kindly hands put out to waylay and assist her, lungs scorched with acrid fumes, throat raw and agonizing. On and on she ran, weaving her way back and forth across the road in her bare feet as though to escape the memories which would be with her for life.

Twin blossoms of orange light flowered in front of her, grew larger, screamed to a halt. There were more voices, the banging of car doors and then, incredibly, Martin's voice: "Celia! Oh thank God! Whatever happened? Are you hurt?"

With his arms supporting her she turned at last to look back. Along the road the sky was lit with a lurid orange glow and flame-streaked smoke poured up into the darkness with a scattering of sparks falling from it like miniature shooting stars. Two fire-engines, sirens screaming discordantly, sped past them. Martin said urgently, "What happened? Did you get out in time?"

She nodded, teeth chattering ferociously. "Eva and Lucas are still inside."

She heard his sharply indrawn breath and felt, with gratitude, the rough tweed of his coat, warm from his body, go round her cold shoulders.

"I was frantic when Mother said you'd phoned. I'd gone to London to get Bishop Langley." He half-turned to the man standing behind him. "Celia, you are sure you're all right?"

"Yes. They gave me something to drink. I don't know

212

what it was but it slowed down my reactions. I didn't realize
the danger until it was almost too late. I tried to drag Eva
out—her hair was on fire—but she dodged back to Lucas.
Martin, it was horrible! They were both so drugged they
didn't know what was happening. There were black draperies over everything, and candles. They opened the window
because I was so hot. It was the wind that caused the fire.
My fault!" She began to sob helplessly and his arms went
clumsily round her.

An elderly voice somewhere behind her said with quiet
authority, "Martin, will you take Mrs. Bannerman home
before she catches a chill? And I think a doctor ought to see
her hands as soon as possible. I'll go and find that policeman
who passed us and give him such details as are necessary.
She'll probably have to make a statement later but until we
know what they found up there—" His voice trailed off
uncertainly.

The rest of that gruesome night was afterwards recalled
only by a series of tableaux: the drive home with Martin,
Tom's horrified face and Mrs. Bannerman's quick, gentle
hands; her warm bed and Alan bending over her, bandaging
her blistered hands. Then, at last, total unconsciousness,
unlit by dreams of any kind, which lasted a full sixteen hours
until lunch time the following day.

Soon afterwards a police inspector, grave and sympathetic,
came to hear her account of the fire. Primed by Martin, Celia
said merely that she was at the flat with a couple of friends
when the fire broke out with such suddenness they had no
hope of escape.

The man leant forward, pencil poised. "Ah yes, that's one
point we want to clear up. I believe you told the men first on
the scene that there were two people upstairs?"

"That's right."

213

"You're sure of that?"

She stared at him with a frown. "Of course I'm sure. Why?"

"Because we found only one body, ma'am. When it was possible to get into the building we came across the badly charred body of a girl. Nothing else. I believe she was a relative of some kind? Please accept my sympathy."

"Thank you," Celia said mechanically. "But—that's not possible. Mr. Todd was there too." She swallowed, wincing at the pain in her throat. "He's the music master at my husband's school."

"The occupant of the flat? Yes, we learned that a Mr. Todd leased it at the beginning of September but so far we have been unable to trace him and, of course, the flat was completely gutted. Nothing remained at all. It was a terrible business."

"Terrible," Celia repeated tremblingly.

"One thing that puzzles us is how it took hold so fast."

"It was the draught from the window—and all the candles."

"Ah yes. Unfortunately fire is always a hazard at this time of the year. Candles and paper decorations—it takes very little to send the whole lot up." He closed his notebook. "Then you can't help us as to the whereabouts of Mr. Todd?"

"He was definitely there. With Eva."

"Then we can only assume he somehow made his escape, though it hardly seems possible. Some of the men forced an entry by way of the fire escape but they didn't see anyone leave, and the ceiling came down before those who passed you could get up the stairs. Also, you'd think he if did escape he'd have contacted us."

Celia had another visitor that day. Just as darkness was falling, Tom tapped on her door and announced in a rather

214

awed voice that Bishop Langley had called to see her. She turned as the distinguished figure entered behind him and held out her bandaged hand. He took it gently and sat down beside her. Tom, after a moment's hesitation, left them alone.

"It was good of you to come."

"I felt I must have a word with you before I returned to London, if only to satisfy myself that you really have escaped unscathed."

"Martin told you everything?"

"Yes, a most disturbing story. We can only thank God it ended as it did."

She said slowly, "It's odd, you know. He was so strong, so powerful. It seems incredible that a tiny thing like a candle could cause his downfall."

The Bishop smiled slightly, his stern face becoming warmer. "Don't you think, my dear, that perhaps you are rather underestimating the Almighty?"

She stared at him blankly.

"Oh ye of little faith!" he chided her gently. "Miracles don't always occur with a clap of thunder, you know! A candle is quite sufficient to work God's will." And, as she continued to gaze at him unspeaking, he added, "Can you deny that the fire occurred only just in time? That it destroyed all that was evil and yet left you unharmed? Wasn't it, in fact, just the deliverance we were all praying so hard for? If that isn't a miracle, I don't know what more you want!"

Hadn't Eva said something similar? *It must all seem perfectly natural.* Perhaps good and evil moved in the same mysterious ways. Tears of weakness and relief filled her eyes and began to spill down her cheeks.

"I won't tire you," the Bishop said quietly, "but perhaps

we might just have a short prayer together before I go, to give thanks for your deliverance."

And this time, as his quiet voice washed over her, the words of praise and thanksgiving seeped gently through into her understanding, comforting, soothing away the horrors and traumas of the last few months.

He stood and patted her hand. "God bless you and keep you, my dear, and a happy Christmas to you and your family."

She could not reply. The sense of overwhelming peace was too new, too precious. *You and your family.* They were safe, together still. How could she have doubted it was a miracle?

As for Lucas Todd, his whereabouts were to remain an unsolved mystery on the files of Rychester Constabulary. Occasionally—though she thought of him less and less—Celia wondered how the local police would react if she were to offer them what she believed to be his present address.